Transient Beings

Also by Patrick Semple

A Parish Adult Education Handbook – Editor

Believe It Or Not – A Memoir

That Could Never Be – with K Dalton

The Rectory Dog – Poetry Collection

The Rector Who Wouldn't Pray For Rain – A Memoir

A Narrow Escape – Poetry Collection

TRANSIENT BEINGS

Patrick Semple

Code Green Publishing

ISBN 978-1-907215-18-6

Version 1.0

Cover design by Code Green Publishing

Published by
Code Green Publishing
Coventry, England

www.codegreenpublishing.com

For all long-suffering country rectors.

CHAPTER 1

'It's all very well for you,' Jennifer would say, 'I know you once worked in a bank, but you were brought up on a farm so you know the ways of these country bumpkins.'

Jennifer, a city girl, and I had met at university where she read mathematics, which she said sarcastically was the perfect preparation to be the wife of a country clergyman. She would then add that it was, in fact, beyond the capacity of human ingenuity to prepare any person for that role; one had to learn to go under on the job!

In the early years of our marriage Jennifer tried to do what was expected of her as a clergyman's wife, even when most of her time was taken up with the children. People expected her always to be in good humour, welcome them when they called to the door and offer tea or coffee and sit and chat for as long as they wanted to stay. All of this regardless of what she was doing in the house at the time. She had, however, long since abandoned any attempt to meet parishioners' expectations of any kind; in fact nowadays she took little part in the parish at all and went to church only when she wanted to and that was not often.

I had no difficulty with her sitting lightly to the parish. I respected her right to be her own person, and to make her own decisions. It surprised me in the early days that she was prepared to do so much of what was expected of her, but she did it for my sake. As she said herself she didn't want parishioners saying: 'The poor unfortunate man married to that woman who does nothing to help him.' She would not mind being referred to as 'that woman,' but she would hate to think I might be referred to as 'the poor unfortunate man.'

Jennifer answered the phone in the hall as I came down the stairs. She put her hand over the mouthpiece.

'It's Mrs Bowers.'

I grimaced and took the receiver. 'Hello.' I wedged the handset between my jaw and shoulder, took out my glasses and checked my diary for the day.

'Why can't you ask him yourself?' I asked her, trying to conceal my impatience, 'or ask him to meet you and let you take the jars.' I put away my diary and glasses and straightened the notepad on the table.

'I know he guards the boiler house jealously, but there's been so much trouble about the key recently he's reluctant to let it out of his sight, but he will if you promise to bring it straight back to him.'

'Your breakfast is on the table,' Jennifer called from the kitchen.

'All right then, I'll ask him to leave the jars in the church,' I said, struggling to be polite, and I put down the phone.

'The bitch,' I muttered under my breath as I crossed the hall to the kitchen.

'What's biting her now?' asked Jennifer.

'She won't ask Bob for the key of the boiler house to get out some jars for flowers. That's at least twice this week that she's tried my patience.'

'It's a small price to pay for all the work she does around the parish,' Jennifer said.

'I know. She does a great deal of good and then ruins it all by being awkward or saying something bitter or cantankerous; she's like a cow that gives a good bucket of milk and kicks it over, and you know who has to mop it up.'

Jennifer had my boiled egg ready on the table in the middle of the kitchen. She had already had her own breakfast, which never amounted to more than a mug or two of black coffee that she drank standing with her back to the cooker, her dressing-gown tied tightly around her and smoking a cigarette. I sat to the table from where I could see the green haze on the big beech tree. When it came into full leaf it would shade the far end of what had once been a croquet lawn. The children's swing still hung from one of its branches.

There had been a frost overnight, the sun was up and the sky was deep blue and crystal clear. The kind of morning, I mused, that should not be allowed in Lent, but should be compulsory after Easter.

The rectory was a mile from the village. Nobody knew why it had been built so far from the church; probably because in the early nineteenth century the parish had owned the piece of land, and even for the Church economic factors are those most likely to influence decisions. The convenience of the rector would have been secondary, especially if at the time he had not been a member of the local gentry. In the 1970s, a century and a half later, I was particularly glad the house was far enough from the village to give us some privacy.

The entrance was neglected. Giant beech trees, the best part of a hundred years old, towered above it. Some of them were so close to the back of the curved walls that they had dislodged coping-stones, allowing frost to open large cracks and in one place to collapse the wall altogether. The rusted gates had not been used for a long time; both were off their swivels. One was still held more or less upright by the eye at the top while the other had fallen back onto the verge and was only partially visible in the grass that had been growing through it for years. The sporadic efforts of a succession of rectors to keep the area around the house itself had not extended to the entrance where moss and weeds completed the picture of dereliction.

The avenue, lined by a barbed wire fence on both sides maintained by the farmer who rented the glebe land, divided near the house; the right branch of the fork led to the stable-yard through two cut-limestone pillars. The other branch of the fork on the avenue led to the house. It opened out into a sweep that faced rich grassland, with a line of low hills in the distance. There were steps to the hall door with a window on either side and three

4

windows above. It was the kind of house that Jennifer, from middle-class Dublin, and I, from a long line of yeoman farmers, would never have had the opportunity to live in if it hadn't been tied to the job. It had been built as a rectory and had been one ever since.

The whole atmosphere of the place was a reminder of a bygone era, a time when the local rector was a member of the ascendancy and his Church was the established Church; when the majority of the local population were members of what their masters sometimes referred to offensively as the Roman Mission in Ireland. After Catholic Emancipation and in due course the formation of the State, this juxtaposition of the two Churches was reversed. Subsequently, after the Second Vatican Council, both traditions began to work with, rather than against, each other and on both sides to heal the hurts of the past.

Inside the house were a large drawing-room and an almost equally large dining-room. They were rooms of their period, finely proportioned with high ceilings and difficult to heat. The kitchen in the basement had been abandoned some years before and a modern kitchen had been made in what had formerly been a breakfast or morning-room. Surprisingly for a house of its size, it had only four bedrooms, and one of these had been turned into a bathroom. It was a delightful house to live in, and no doubt when it was built there were at least three indoor and two or three outdoor staff but, despite modern appliances that replaced the human hand, it was hard to keep.

Jennifer and I had no private means, but we did not complain since we were happy to live in whatever house went with the job, within reason; especially since the children had grown and gone. Shortly after we arrived in the parish the vestry had installed central heating, but we had the feeling that some parishioners thought that this was an extravagance that many of them didn't have themselves.

The parish was rural, with the main church in the village and two outlying churches. It was a tillage area with a fair proportion of prosperous farmers. Most of the parishioners made their living, one way or another, from agriculture; one was a shopkeeper in the village and a few worked in the nearest town eight miles away. There was one 'big house' where the direct line would soon die out. The present owner, Robert Armstrong, a bachelor in his late seventies, at one time attended church regularly and had been a member of the vestry and involved himself in the day-to-day affairs of the parish. In recent years he attended church only occasionally; he was no longer elected onto the vestry but kept an eye on parochial affairs from a distance. This interest was less from concern for the parish than to maintain the family tradition according to which he believed everything in the area, especially the parish, had its origins in the Armstrong family. This may well have been true in the seventeenth century when his Cromwellian ancestors had been allocated a large tract of land as a reward for loyal military service. These days the only thing, apart from his house and a small amount of remaining land, over which he felt he could exercise any influence, was the parish, and even that was waning. He had no residual influence over the people of the village or the families of the former Armstrong tenants.

Jennifer was still talking about Mrs Bowers:

'If you let her torment you,' she said, 'it's your own fault.'

'She does torment me. It's all right for you, you don't have to deal with her the way I do; anyway I wasn't thinking about her. Where were you last night? You were late again. I didn't hear you coming in.'

'At Kate's. You were sound asleep.' There followed a long silence during which I decided that it was not a good time to pursue any further the subject of Jennifer's late hours.

'How's Kate?' I asked.

'She's fine. You know Siobhán is making her First Holy Communion next term. Kate was at the parents' night recently and found it hard on her own.'

Jennifer and I met Kate after her husband, Conor, eloped with a parishioner of mine. Father Keane, the parish priest, was a kindly elderly gentleman who didn't quite know what to say or do at the time, especially as Kate was one of his primary schoolteachers. Kate, for her part, felt that Father Keane somehow blamed her and she was sure that some of the parents did. She could not work out why this might be so, especially as she knew nothing of the affair until the day before Conor left. People didn't know who to blame and the Protestant/Catholic thing added another dimension to the blame game.

Kate had come to the rectory early on to talk to me, and she and Jennifer hit it off immediately. Kate was devastated and for months she was too numb even to talk much, but she would come and sit and make the odd comment and then slowly she began to articulate what she felt. I had no doubt that, as a woman, Jennifer could be of more help to her than I could and as time passed this proved to be the case so that she came to talk to Jennifer and a firm friendship was established between them. It was over two years since Kate's husband had left and she had worked out a new routine. She still called to the rectory to see Jennifer, and Jennifer often went down to Kate at night when I was out, and sometimes when I wasn't.

'We must be sure to get something for Siobhán's First Holy Communion,' I said, 'it will be hard for her without her Dad.'

By now Jennifer was sitting sideways on to me between the cooker and the end of the table, her heels on the top rung of the stool, her arms resting on her knees and holding her coffee mug. She was staring at the top of the cooker in the way people stare into a fire and I wondered what she was thinking. Her unkempt red hair had more grey in it than I had noticed before. When I met her first I once referred to her as a raspberry brunette.

'I'm a red head,' she retorted crossly, which I discovered was typical of her.

I looked at Jennifer perched on her stool; she had lost weight. I remembered her in college when we first started going out together: ponytail, chunky sweater and jeans, with her books and everything else except the kitchen sink in a hessian bag with 'MAKE LOVE NOT WAR' on it. She was an active member of the Students' Union and an avid participant in student causes and protests. I envied the freedom she had to live student life to the full while I had commitments at the theological college.

When we moved to the country first she found it lonely but her facility for making friends soon helped her to settle in.

'What's on to-day?' I asked.

'I'm going to write to the children; I owe them both a letter, and after lunch I have some things I want in the village.'

'I'm going out now and I'll be back for lunch,' I said, and left the kitchen with Jennifer still perched on the stool with her hands wrapped around the empty mug.

CHAPTER 2

In the past the Armstrong family saw the parish as part of their estate rather than the estate as part of the parish. Robert Armstrong still felt something of this, despite the fact that the family had been reduced to one, and that now his connection with the parish was tenuous. The family had built the church in the village; their coat of arms was over the door outside and on the walls inside the church there were memorial tablets to generations of Armstrongs.

The house was Georgian and as grand houses go it was in moderate condition. You came upon it quite suddenly around a sharp curve on the lime tree avenue. It was a square block of a house with no distinguishing features, but nobody had interfered with the façade since it was built.

Inside, the house was a classic specimen of shabby gentility. Soft furnishings were threadbare and dirty, much of the furniture needed re-upholstering or repair and a thick layer of dust covered everything. An old fashioned telephone was the only modern item in the house. Bill was the sole member of staff. He was a gentleman's gentleman who had been trained by his father who in his turn had fulfilled that role for Mr Armstrong's father, the old Colonel. 'Duggan,' as Mr Armstrong called Bill, did everything. He was butler, cook, housemaid, footman and general factotum all rolled into one. He filtered callers to the house, he did the shopping, cooked and served meals, he looked after the fuel and the fire in the study, the only room in the house that could be made warm and comfortable in winter. He wore an old dinner jacket and grey flannel bags, except when he was serving meals to Mr Armstrong, seated at the end of the long table in the dining room, when Bill wore a short white jacket for all the world like a barber or hospital porter.

Mr Armstrong didn't phone the rectory often. This was the first time he had phoned and asked me to call. As I drove up the avenue I wondered what could be the reason for the summons, but found it hard to think since all my concentration was needed to negotiate the potholes which, if planned, could not have been more awkwardly placed. I arrived at the basement door and found Bill in the kitchen.

'Hello, your reverence, great weather.'

'Hello, Bill how are you?'

'He's above in the study, I'll take you up.'

The 'he' rather than 'Mr Armstrong' or 'the master,' was not a disloyalty but a way of ingratiating himself with me. Bill, a bachelor, didn't fraternize in the village and was known only from his visits to the shops. Older villagers did remember him from school, but since his mother, who had also worked at the big house, died he became even more reclusive and nobody knew if he had any other relatives or where his family had come from.

Bill took off his apron and led me up the back stairs, through the dining-room and the saloon to the study door. He knocked, and a voice from inside said:

'Yes.'

Bill pushed open the door and said:

'His reverence is here.'

Mr Armstrong stood up from the desk and Bill disappeared. 'Ah, rector, come in.' Neither of them ever used my name.

Robert Armstrong, somewhere in his mid-seventies, was of medium height; thin grey hair brushed flat, round face, keen grey eyes and sallow complexion. Apart from rare formal occasions when he wore a suit, I never saw him in anything other than the same pale-coloured Harris Tweed jacket, with a working handkerchief stuffed into the top pocket, thick twills and collar and tie. He moved a tin deed box off a button-back armchair for me to sit down. Every surface, including chairs, was covered with papers, maps and books. These were all the stock-in-trade of his full-time occupation: ensuring the survival of the house and what was left of the estate. There were miniatures and silhouettes on both sides of the fireplace and hunting prints on the other walls. There was a bowler hat and crop on top of a large glass-fronted bookcase.

Mr Armstrong went to a cupboard in the corner and produced a bottle of sherry and two glasses. No matter what time of day I visited the house he brought out the sherry. This time, at eleven o'clock in the morning, I didn't particularly want it but it was easier to take it. He poured the sherry and without any further preliminaries he came straight to the point.

'What plans have you got to mark the hundred and fiftieth anniversary of the parish church? I have the original papers here; the service of dedication was held on 15th October one hundred and fifty years ago this year.'

'I haven't begun to think about it yet,' I said, which wasn't strictly true. I had thought about it but I had purposely done nothing. I knew it was the one hundred and fiftieth year of the church, but I hoped nobody would notice. I had an aversion to festivals and celebrations. I neither liked to organize them nor did I like the prominent position that inevitably I had to take in them. The Sunday services and the seasonal services of the Church were plenty for me and if I had my way there would be fewer of them too. I never liked dressing up and parading; I was tense and nervous taking the routine Sunday services even after all these years, let alone conducting services on special occasions.

'Have you something in mind?' I asked.

'Well, before we do anything the church needs to be re-decorated. Some guttering and downpipes need to be replaced and that damaged yew inside the gate will have to be taken away.' He was right, all these things did need to be done, but resentment welled up inside me, that although he seldom came near the parish, he was making plans for the church. This was not to the glory of

God, or even of the parish, but for the aggrandisement of his family name.

He went on: 'The main event should be an ecumenical service of thanksgiving,' (not to God, I thought, but to the Armstrongs!), 'with all the local and neighbouring clergy present. The bishop of course will attend and preach.' (The gentry like bishops to officiate at their family liturgical occasions, and bishops usually do.) 'The school can do something for the children and the different parish groups can put on events of their own.'

I was astounded that he had been thinking about this; planning what should happen and presenting it to me as a *fait accompli*. My resentment turned to anger, which I was not prepared to let him see.

'And what will you do?' I asked as calmly as I could.

'I will pay for the redecoration and other work to the church and give the parish two hundred and fifty pounds to make a jolly good festival. As far as possible we should involve the whole community over the period of a week.'

I was dumbfounded. Such generosity was out of character and wanting the whole community to be involved didn't fit either, since he didn't take any part in the local community; in fact they used to say he didn't even buy his petrol in the village. Once he had made such a generous offer I knew I had no way out; if the vestry heard that I had turned down two hundred and fifty pounds there'd be hell to pay.

'I'll have to give it some thought,' I said, wanting to hold the initiative and without commenting on or thanking him for his offer I stood up and turned towards the door. He followed and having, as he saw it, had his own way, he indulged that gentry facility for trivial conversation as he walked me to my car.

Furious, and going over the conversation in my head, I drove into every pothole on the avenue.

'The bastard' I said over and over again, 'he's not going to bully me.'

I would decide, with the parish, how to celebrate one hundred and fifty years of the church, but I knew I could not pass up free decoration and repairs, and two hundred and fifty pounds. I could of course, but if I did the parishioners would be confirmed in their view that I didn't live in quite the same world as they did. By the time I reached the road I realised that Mr Armstrong's offer, as far as I was concerned, amounted to bribery.

I drove back to the rectory, went straight to the kitchen and made a mug of coffee. I sat looking out the window trying to calm myself. I knew I shouldn't let the bugger bother me, but he did. I watched a thrush with nesting material entering the hedge at the end of the garden. I envied him. He had a job to do and without being accountable to anyone he was getting on with it, following his instinct to procreate the next generation. I looked forward to hearing his incomparable song during the long evenings as much as I dreaded the prospect of the anniversary celebrations. I had become angry because I felt guilty about not making some plan myself, and now I had been upstaged and the whole thing was going to become the kind of circus I dreaded.

Jennifer came downstairs.

'You're back. What did he want?' I told her.

'Well I think it'll be fun. You're such a stick-in-the-mud. We need something to liven things up. Nothing happens around here but people living out their boring little lives day in day out, with nothing to look forward to apart from a week in a caravan at the sea or a day at the races. The Prods are so dull and respectable; most of them are afraid to enjoy themselves for fear their Catholic neighbours might discover they're human.'

'Would you mind telling me what the purpose of a festival, or whatever you want to call it, is?' I asked.

'It's an opportunity to celebrate. It's an excuse for a party, and a hundred and fifty years of the church is as good a reason as any. It doesn't matter what the reason, anything will do so long as it puts a bit of life into the place, and it's an ideal opportunity for people to do things together.'

'It'll be ironic for the Catholic clergy who take part,' I said, 'in a service of thanksgiving for the building of a church by people who at the time were enforcing draconian laws that made the practice of their own religion illegal. They drove their predecessors to the forests and the hills to say mass, in an attempt to force one interpretation of the Christian faith on the people.'

'Oh, for God's sake nobody will see it like that. Father Keane is much too kindly and Christian a man to even think of it.'

'I know he is, but it's ironic none the less. I'm not too happy about celebrating some of the attitudes that emanated from that church over the last hundred and fifty years. It was built on the backs of the poor and dispossessed and it was the spiritual focus that buttressed years of repression. I never cease to marvel at how forgiving Irish Catholic country people are, and how tolerant they are of the descendants of those who kept them down for so long.'

'Are you finished?' asked Jennifer. 'That's all history, and we have to move on. We all did terrible things to each other in the past, but thank goodness we've all got sense and these days we're working together. What's all that to do with having a bit of a party?'

'I don't want to think about it now,' I said. 'I'll have a vestry meeting after Easter and see what they think we ought to do. They'll have to do something if they're to have the church repaired and decorated free to the parish. "Money talks" is true nowhere more than in a select vestry.'

'Kate phoned while you were out.' Jennifer said as she lifted the saucepan lid and poked the potatoes. 'She's coming this afternoon; she wants to talk to you about Siobhán's First Holy Communion. She's going to ask you if she can send her to your school.'

'Of course she can, if that's what she wants to do, but Siobhán should make her Communion first.'

'That's what she wants to avoid, but she'll tell you the story herself.'

'By the way,' I asked, 'who was that young man that drove out just as I came to the entrance?'

'What young man? I don't know,' Jennifer replied.

'The young man who drove out the entrance. He drove the other way just as I slowed down to turn in.'

'I've no idea, I didn't hear a car. Nobody called.'

After lunch I went into the study and closed the door. I sat at the desk in front of a pile of papers and letters that had needed my attention for a long time. Resting my arms on the desk I propped my chin in my hands and looked at the photograph of Jennifer with our children when they were small. It rubbed my nose in the passage of time, and reminded me that Jennifer's only real purpose since the children were grown and gone was to keep house and be the rector's wife, neither of which she took seriously. She did as much of these as she wanted to, but lately she was spending more and more time out of the house.

I was always low at this time of the year, and Lent and all that it meant didn't help. I had no stomach for work, but felt a strong urge to get away and clear my head, but it wasn't possible. I knew it would pass, as it always did, but not before I had agonized again about whether I should be in the job at all or not. I seldom thought I wanted to throw the whole thing over, but there was a great deal about the job and the teaching of the Church that I found hard to take. There was nobody I could talk to except Jennifer, and what she believed didn't seem to bother her. She thought I was making too much of the business of belief. She said the parish was simply a way for me to work with people, which she would like to have done herself. She didn't know any theology, but didn't consider that a handicap in having an opinion on everything to do with the Church and Christianity.

I knew that if I went to see the bishop, when he eventually had time to see me, he would utter a few platitudes to say that everybody, modestly including himself, had doubts from time to time. He would tell me about some black patch he went through when he was in Kilbrian, where he was for twenty something years and which he never stopped quoting; 'When I was in Kilbrian.......' He would probably go on to tell me that all the great saints of the Church had dark nights of the soul, failing to notice that I was hardly a candidate to be numbered amongst them but saying: 'If the saints had doubts it's not surprising that you do.' He would talk about himself and the abstract problem of doubt and then without taking me as a person and my particular concern seriously, he would probably patronize me by patting me metaphorically on the head and saying that, like a cold, it would pass.

If I went to the bishop I would come away feeling misunderstood or even pitied but certainly not having been taken seriously. I would have more respect for the man if he referred me to someone who knew some theology to discover if I should resign or not. I didn't want to go to him now. Easter was coming up, then summer with my usual month's holiday, followed by whatever it was we were going to do for the centenary of the church, and then before the winter if I still felt the same I might do something.

Nobody knows what anybody else believes unless they actually declare it. People assume that clergy and regular churchgoers believe the orthodox Christian faith as laid out in the creeds, but in my experience most people don't actually own for themselves a particular faith. Most parishioners accept on trust the teaching of the Church without knowing fully what it is that they are subscribing to. In many ways they think the clergy understand and believe it all vicariously for them, and all they have to do is turn up and take part.

There are of course some who reflect upon and struggle with the issues of belief themselves. Some of these are particularly zealous and certainly own their beliefs, and they're often a damn nuisance to the clergy, because they're likely to hold opinions about how things should be done in the parish that don't fit in with the rector. There are others who hold opinions that they don't tell the clergy, perhaps in some cases for fear of shocking them. Some regular churchgoers, for whom churchgoing is important, don't believe in life after death. Their religion is about living in the world, and not about trying to gain access to the next one.

Church membership has become institutionalized and ritualized to the point that the institution and the ritual have become ends in themselves. The Church has thrown a fire blanket over every flame of reason so that members sublimate any difficult question they may have to the will of God. A parishioner once told me that the reason that two young men we both knew were killed in a car crash was because God wanted both of them in heaven. I was more inclined to believe that the reason they were killed was because the driver had had too much to drink and was driving too fast. Such was the kind of gulf between some of my parishioners and me, that I felt it my duty, one way or the other, to try to bridge.

I began to sort the papers on my desk. I filed some away, put some in piles for phone calls or to pass on to other people and some I threw into the wastepaper basket. At this stage of my life I had become ruthless with the junk mail I received from steeplejacks, the healing ministry and some missionary societies. When I was ordained first I kept everything unless there was good reason why I should put it in the wastepaper basket. Nowadays I put everything in the wastepaper basket unless there was good reason why I should keep it – a change of emphasis caused by a weariness with other people dragging out of me.

The doorbell rang. I answered it; it was Kate and Siobhán. There was the subtle scent of the expensive perfume Kate used. When we were married first Jennifer did occasionally use perfume, but was always quick to say it was for her own pleasure. 'Women should dress to please themselves, and not men,' she would say, and carried it out in practice. I don't believe she had used perfume for many years now, even on formal occasions.

Kate was average height, rounded without being plump; comfortable. She smiled readily and she was warm and feminine. Siobhán stood behind Kate holding her mother's hand. At eight it was impossible to know what she thought, and despite my efforts to make friends with her, she kept her distance. It was probably because I was a clergyman, or maybe it was that since she met me first to do with her father leaving, I was, for her, somehow implicated in that, and this despite Kate's friendliness, or maybe even because of it. I had become fond of Kate and admired the plucky way she was coping with her problems.

'Jennifer is in the kitchen,' I said, and Siobhán went ahead of Kate through the hall. 'I'll be there in a little while.'

I went back into the study and sat down again at the desk. I finished sorting the papers and put some for the parish treasurer into an envelope. It was actually possible to administer a parish well and be a successful rector without believing a great deal about the gospel. I knew what I believed and what I didn't, and above all I didn't want to disturb people's faith, but neither did I want to be a hypocrite. I had recently begun to wonder if I was staying because I had no other way to earn a living. I had a good general education with a degree, but in terms of the marketplace I was trained for nothing. Who'd employ a defunct cleric in his late fifties?

I know that if I decided to leave it wouldn't be a problem for Jennifer, but neither of us had the potential to earn a living that would pay even a modest rent. We were married before Jennifer could do a teaching diploma, and the only thing she could do now would be to give grinds in maths. Even with a free house, a clerical stipend and the children financially off our hands we weren't managing very well: Jennifer always seemed to be short of money. She went to one of the pubs in the village for company when I was out at night, and I understood that, but she seemed to spend more money than we could afford, and drank more than I thought was wise.

I had stopped making this point to her since she wasn't able to discuss it or deny it without getting angry and turning it against me.

'If you would only get out of this god-forsaken place at the back end of nowhere, I might be able to get a life. As it is what am I to do?' Then if my challenge had been direct enough she would launch into a counter offensive. 'If you'd make up your mind about what you believe and what you don't, you might have the courage to leave.' Whatever way the discussion went it always turned into an argument in which I was to blame for everything, so I stopped bringing up the problem. When I use that word I can hear her say: 'Problem, what problem? I've no problem. It's you has the problem.'

I took the envelope for the treasurer, put it on the hall table and went out to the kitchen. Siobhán was on the floor playing with a doll from a box of toys Jennifer kept for when children came. Kate and Jennifer were sitting at the table with mugs of coffee exchanging informed female opinions on Kate's school principal, in his fifties, a bachelor and in their expert opinion likely to remain so.

'Maybe he's gay,' I interjected, primarily to get a reaction. There was a short silence that Kate ended with:

'Maybe he is, but I doubt it. If he is, that's his own business and good luck to him, but I wish he'd learn to keep his hands and his suggestive remarks to himself.'

It was clear that that was all they were prepared to say on that particular subject now that I was present, so I asked Kate in a general way how she was.

'Fine!' she said, 'but I'm not happy about this First Communion, although to be fair it's better than it used to be. They don't learn so much by rote any more, and what they do learn has more to do with living in this world than preparing for the next one. It's the whole ritual I don't like.'

'We all need rituals of some kind,' I said, 'it's part of being human, and if we don't use the ones that are there we'll make up our own.'

'I know,' said Kate, 'I think I could buy the ritual if it weren't for everything that went with the day. It's not that I'll be on my own……'

'You won't be on your own,' Jennifer interrupted ' I'll be with you.'

'I know you will,' Kate said, with a smile and a gentleness that showed her appreciation, 'but it's what's spent on clothes and the children collecting money afterwards. It's nothing to do with Christianity, and I feel sorry for parents who can't afford it.'

'You can't blame the Church for that,' I said, 'the priests do the best they can to put a stop to all of that, but most of the parents won't listen.'

I gave a cryptic signal to Jennifer who took Siobhán out to the garden to see if they could see the thrush's nest in the hedge.

'Anyway I'm not happy with Siobhán making her Communion at all.' Kate continued, 'I don't think she's ready and if she doesn't she'll be even more the odd-one-out in her class. What I really want to ask you is, will you take Siobhán in your school? I've never been happy with her in the school where I teach, especially since Conor left.'

I knew from Jennifer that Kate was determined on this course, and while we were always glad of new children to keep the numbers up, I wanted to be sure that she had thought it through.

'By your own admission Siobhán's class teacher is good.'

'She is, but it's more the other children and one or two of the parents. For myself I don't mind remarks and knowing looks, but it's not fair on Siobhán.'

'Won't she miss her friends and with Conor's amour being a Protestant won't people think it strange?' I knew as soon as I said it what Kate's answer would be.

'I don't care what people think so long as it's right for Siobhán, and children make new friends easily at that age.'

It didn't surprise me that Kate had worked it all out, and that she would pursue with determination what she believed was the right course of action. Behind her gentleness there was strength. She had coped admirably with Conor leaving and above all she wanted to protect Siobhán.

'Kate, if you're quite sure, it's fine with me,' I said, 'of course we'll have Siobhán; in fact we can't refuse her if there's room in the school and there's plenty, but would you do something to please me? Will you let her make her First Communion before she moves?'

Kate looked into her coffee mug for a few seconds, then looked me straight in the eye and said gently but firmly: 'No, John, I won't.'

'What can I say? Of course we'll take Siobhán. It's no wonder you and Jennifer get on so well; you're both stubborn.' Kate smiled. 'Jennifer's answer when I accuse her of stubbornness is: "Animals are stubborn, I just know my own mind, which is a virtue in a confused world."'

Kate and I went out to the garden where Jennifer was pushing Siobhán on the swing. 'Did you see the nest?' I asked. Jennifer replied: 'We were afraid to go too close in case she might desert, so we had a swing instead.'

'You three ladies of leisure may have nothing better to do,' I said, 'but I have.' I said good-bye to Kate and Siobhán and went to the study where a shaft of sunlight lit up my desk as if to spotlight the work I had left to do. I chose to ignore this impertinent reminder from nature's source of all life, closed the door, and taking a stick from the stand in the hall, I made for the track behind the house that led to a walk in the forestry beyond.

CHAPTER 3

I had always found Lent difficult. On the few occasions in my life that I had observed Lent rigorously and had endured it, rather than feeling chastened, I was pleased with myself. I felt proud as Punch that I had kept my resolution, and of course pride is the greatest sin of all, especially the pride that apes humility. Apart from this, Lent did nothing for me and I certainly couldn't see how it did anything for God. The great piece of clerical cant is that in Lent we shouldn't give something up, but take up something. Drinking tea is an occupational hazard of clergy, so one Lent I took up abstinence from tea. It was no joke, but I succeeded, and I remember the nectar of my first cup on Easter Sunday morning. A Lent observed gives zest to Easter, even if it's only a cup of tea. It's human to indulge after a period of deprivation. This year we were well into Lent and I hadn't either given up or taken up anything.

Jennifer always observed Lent. She gave up drink. Neither of us drank much until recent years when Jennifer started coming home late from the pub in the village. After the children had left home she spent a good deal of time in the house. She wasn't in the least house-proud; she always said a house was for the convenience of living and not an end in itself to be admired. She read and she enjoyed the garden. When we were married first and she complained of having time on her hands I used to say: 'You could always do a few sums.' I wouldn't dare make a joke like that now. It might have upset some parishioners that Jennifer went into the pub in the village, but it didn't bother me. Jennifer herself had no time for hypocrisy, and didn't feel she was accountable to parishioners for where she went and with whom she spent her time. What did bother me, however, was that recently she was spending more and more time there and I didn't know who she was with.

The one resolve I did have this year was to talk to Jennifer about her drinking. I thought it was a good time to bring the subject up when she was off it. One morning at breakfast when we were having a relaxed conversation about things in general and nothing in particular we mentioned holidays and money, so I took the opportunity.

'We save quite a bit when you're not going into the village at night,' I dropped in casually.

'Do we?' Jennifer replied with a hint of defensiveness in her tone.

'We do, quite a bit,' I said not wanting to get into an argument about money, 'but it's not the money that worries me.'

'It's what your parishioners think of the rector's wife in the pub.'

'Now that's not fair,' I said, and to put her on the back foot before we got to the real topic: 'We've been over that before; and you know I support your right to be yourself and come and go, where and when you like. You're not answerable to parishioners for your social life any more than I am. Some of them may think they have a lien on me but they certainly haven't got one on you. What I want to say is that I think you're drinking too much.'

There was a long silence. Jennifer got up from the table and put some dishes in the sink. She turned on the tap, filled the basin and turning around to face me said:

'So you don't like the company I keep, well let me tell you they're better company than most of your boring parishioners. I'd rather spend ten minutes with any of them than a whole night with most of the respectable Prods around here.'

'It's not the company I object to; it's the amount you drink. It looks as though it's getting out of control.'

'For God's sake how could it be getting out of control, I haven't had a drink since Ash Wednesday.'

'I know, but that doesn't mean anything. Giving it up for Lent is a way of convincing yourself and me that you're not drinking too much, and giving yourself licence to drink what you like the rest of the year.'

'Where did you get that bit of fancy psycho-babble?'

I ignored her question. 'When you are drinking you often come home less than sober.'

'Don't equivocate. Are you saying I come home drunk?'

'Well since you put it like that, yes.'

She turned back to the sink and began to wash the dishes. I brought my mug and plate from the table, put them on the drainboard and stood beside her.

'Jen, I'm not being judgemental, you know that. It's that I'm afraid your drinking is getting out of hand.'

'How can it be getting out of hand when to give it up for Lent doesn't cost me a thought?'

' I don't think that follows.'

'Can we talk about something else?' she said, turning away and drying her hands.

'I'd like you to think about it,' I said.

'As far as I'm concerned there's nothing to think about. I can drink when I want to and not when I don't want to, and I don't see anything wrong with that.'

There was no point in pursuing it any further, and I was about to leave the kitchen when the phone rang in the study. I answered it, still preoccupied with not having made any impression on Jennifer about her drinking. It was Vera Leonard.

'The doctor has just been. Fred's not good.'

'I'll be over right away.' I put down the phone, took my stole and my home communion set and left.

Fred was in his fifties. He was dying of cancer. It was a slow and painful process, and I had been visiting him regularly for months. He had been an active parishioner in a quiet and unassuming way and there was nothing he wouldn't do for his parish. He had been on the vestry for many years and what he didn't know about the parish and everybody in it wasn't worth knowing. His work in the parish, however, was directed to maintaining the status quo. In his farming he was as up to date as any: he had all the latest machinery and employed all the most modern methods. He used to joke that the day wasn't far off when he'd be able to run the farm from the kitchen with a computer and video screen.

In the parish, however, Fred was against change. When the new liturgies were introduced he opposed them, and I was wasting my time commenting that I noticed he wasn't using seventeenth century implements on his farm and why should the Church use seventeenth century liturgies as implements of worship? The most he ever said in response to this kind of argument was that because everything else in the world was changing so fast, the Church should stay the same. He wasn't the only one in the parish who resisted the new services, but he reluctantly tolerated them in the hope it would keep the young people involved.

Like most people of his generation Fred had a simple faith based on scripture and Church teaching that he had learned as a child. God was up there looking down day and night, and if you were honest and good he would reward you, and if you weren't he would punish you. As he saw it Protestants had a simple faith based on the bible, while Catholics believed a whole lot of things that weren't necessary. This, however, made not a whit of difference to his living and working with his Catholic neighbours, and there was nobody in the countryside he wouldn't help if they were in trouble. He had the greatest respect for Catholics and they for him, but his only fear as his children were growing up was that either of them would marry one, in particular his son. If his son married a Catholic his grandchildren would be Catholic and the farm that had been in his family for generations would go out of Protestant hands. As it transpired both his children did marry Protestants and his son's wife was expecting her first child, which he hoped would be a boy and secure the farm for another generation. He blamed mixed marriages for the decline in Protestant numbers and used to say: 'If we're not careful there won't be a Protestant in the countryside in a couple of generations.'

As I drove up the long narrow avenue that led to the yard at the back of Leonards' house I was more anxious for Vera than I was for Fred. She once told me with admiration that Fred never left the bedroom in the morning without kneeling down beside his bed to say his prayers, and I could believe it. What his prayers were nobody could know but it would not have surprised me if they were the same prayers he had said when he was a child.

I pushed open the back door and went through the back hall past the shoes and wellington boots and heavy-duty outdoor clothes. There was nobody in the kitchen, which was the only modern room in the house. I went through to the front hall. The rest of the house had the atmosphere of fifty or sixty years before; dark colours, varnished and grained woodwork, and threadbare carpets. The profits from the good years for agriculture had gone back into the farm.

I met Vera coming down the stairs. She beckoned me into the sitting room, which was used only at Christmas and for weddings and funerals, and closed the door. She looked frail and wan.

'He's low, and sleeping most of the time.'

'What did the doctor say?'

'That he'll need a nurse at night. He's bringing up a lot of phlegm and needs to be lifted.' Vera led the way upstairs and into the half-darkened bedroom. Fred was propped up on a heap of pillows, his eyes closed. He didn't hear us coming in so we stood for a few moments and listened to his laboured breathing. Vera put her hand on his hand but he didn't stir. She put her hand on his shoulder and shook him gently:

'The rector's here to see you.' He opened his eyes and said something I couldn't hear. He had failed noticeably in the few days since I had seen him last.

'How are things, Fred?' I asked.

'Not so rosy at the moment,' he whispered slowly. I held his farmer's leathery hand that was now no more than skin and bone.

'Are you comfortable?' I asked, and before he could answer Vera levered him forward and began to fix the pillows behind him. I helped from the other side and Vera laid him back gently.

'Would you like communion?' I asked, and before he could answer he began to cough. Vera took the lid off the yoghurt carton on the bedside locker, held him up and with a deep productive 'hock' he spat into it. She wiped his mouth with a tissue and laid him back onto the pillows. He lay there looking straight ahead till his breathing slowed, and then said:

'I'm not prepared. Could you come to-morrow?' Despite being close to death, he could not break the habit of a lifetime and take communion without preparing himself. His God expected discipline before dispensing grace.

'Of course I can, I'll come in the morning.'

He closed his eyes and appeared to drift into sleep. I waited and watched the slow ebbing of a good life. Fred was an honourable man who put into practice in his daily living what he believed. I couldn't for the life of me understand why he should die so young. In a few minutes I stood up and administered the blessing, and Vera came downstairs with me. We went into the sitting room again.

'He may not last until morning,' Vera said realistically, and her eyes filled up.

'It's hard on you, I'm sure you're not getting much sleep, but it will help when Bernie is here at night,' I said, trying to say something useful, and knowing that there was nothing I could say to relieve her pain. I put my hand on her shoulder and squeezed gently.

'Thank you,' she said, as I turned to leave.

I sat into my car in the yard, more than usually aware of my own physical well-being. I surprised myself at how strongly I thought that I was glad that I was not the one upstairs in that bed waiting to die. I had no fear of death despite not having any idea what lay beyond it, if anything, but about dying I wasn't so sure. It had always seemed to me that there were two main options for dying; prolonged and often painful and degrading, or sudden. I sometimes fantasized about the former when I would have warning and the opportunity to thank Jennifer for everything and to pass on some noble sentiments to the children, but I didn't relish the prospect of pain. To die suddenly would suit me better, but I didn't like the idea that it might be undignified, like dropping dead in a supermarket or falling downstairs and ending up in a heap in the hall.

When confronted with death I always felt inadequate, and not a little hypocritical. At the time of death people placed such confidence in the clergy that extended further than what to do and how to run a funeral service. They particularly wanted the funeral to conform to local custom in order not to give rise to gossip among the neighbours. At this stage of my life, on balance, I didn't believe there was anything after death, but I didn't give a hint of that lest it interfere with the comfort a family might have from the funeral service and its hope of 'a joyful reunion in the heavenly places.' I did, however, suspect that some people believed as I did, but assumed that as I conducted the burial service I believed it all. There is a conspiracy of silence concerning this and many other things that the Church teaches and that people don't believe. Some parishioners however, believe that clergy know all and believe all; they understand Christianity as a package that the clergy can unwrap and dispense to them bit by bit as they need it, and when they have difficulties and doubts the clergy will believe on their behalf.

With this confusion of thoughts going around in my head I started the engine and drove slowly out of the yard. I felt the security of the car that was taking me away from the expectations of people who were facing the inevitable; expectations that were not spoken but implied and therefore impossible to meet; expectations for answers where there are none. Once more I felt the Church was disingenuous in not helping people to face up to the real questions of life and death, but fed them pap that was deficient in the real nourishment they needed to help them face honestly the ultimate mystery.

When I arrived home Jennifer was on the phone in the hall. I heard her say:

'He's just coming in the door.' She covered the mouthpiece and said: 'It's Mrs Bowers.'

'Tell her to go to hell and stop annoying me,' I spat. 'I have more on my mind than flower jars.'

I went into the study. I heard Jennifer saying: 'He says you're to ….,' and for a split second I thought she was going to, '....phone him back in about an hour, he's busy at present.' At that moment I didn't really care if she had said it to her. Jennifer put down the phone and came into the study.

'What's wrong with you?' she asked.

'I've just been to Leonards. Fred is on the way out. That man has more goodness in his little finger than I have in my whole body. What did she want?'

'She didn't say.'

'A bloody state secret. I wish to God she'd stop tormenting me about flowerpots and keys.'

'Jars,' Jennifer corrected. She was always more likely to engage than back off on the rare occasions when I was cross. 'She's a lonely old woman,' she added.

'I know she's a lonely old woman, and I'm not proud of myself, but she'd try the patience of a saint, and I'm not one. She won't phone back; she knows damned well she's tormenting me, but she'll corner me tonight after the service when there are other people around. She's as cunning as a bag of foxes.'

Jennifer, who knew I was patient with Mrs Bowers most of the time, left.

I sat and looked out the window at the clouds and the pink hue in the sky beyond them. Cirrus was the only cloud type I remembered from geography class at school. Neither could I remember the verse about a red sky that told you which way round was good for the shepherd or the sailor. In theory I knew it was as important to care for Mrs Bowers as it was to care for Fred Leonard, but in practice I found it difficult. Fred approaching death asked for nothing; Mrs Bowers in the whole of her health, demanded a lot of attention, and if she didn't use flower jars to get it she used something else.

We observed Lent in the parish with a mid-week service on Wednesday nights. It used to be the custom to have a visiting preacher, but recently with the scarcity of clergy this was harder to arrange, which suited me well, because I preferred to preach myself. I couldn't be sure that a visiting preacher mightn't promote some kind of theology that would confound some of the things I had been trying to drip-feed for years.

Mid-week Lenten services attracted less than a quarter of the Sunday congregation. People who attended sometimes complained about those who didn't, and some of those who didn't made excuses. As far as I was concerned membership of the Church and attendance at services were voluntary. There was no point in people coming to church to please me or to be seen by the neighbours if it was more honest to stay away. Parishioners were shocked when I told them this; they expected me to flatter, cajole or persuade them to attend. For many of them, attending church had little enough to do with Christianity. It had more to do with belonging; belonging to a tribe, in this case a minority tribe, and affirming membership by attending the weekly ritual. The content of the ritual, and its implications for life out in the world, did not seem to be the important things. What was important was that I, the tribal priest, conducted the ritual and that it was performed at the tribal shrine where their forefathers had worshipped before them. Some of these forefathers were commemorated on plaques on the walls of the church and buried in the churchyard – a form of ancestor worship.

These were good people, but nobody challenged them about what they believed, and when I did, many of them resented it or gave me a fool's pardon. They saw it as their duty to clock in and pay up and it was my duty to do the rest; to keep the show on the road and especially not to let the side down against the majority tribe.

I followed Jennifer out to the kitchen and set the table while she took the dinner from the oven. I never felt more like a drink in my life, and went to the cupboard and poured myself a glass of whiskey and added water from the tap. I didn't offer Jennifer anything; she didn't mind me having a drink during Lent when she was off it, but didn't like me drawing attention to it by offering her something else. Furthermore I didn't want another episode like the one in the morning when I tried to talk to her about her drinking. Between Mrs Bowers and herself I'd had enough aggravation for one day.

'How bad is Fred?' Jennifer asked.

'I really don't know. He mightn't survive the night or he might go on for weeks. I really don't know.'

CHAPTER 4

It was breakfast on Easter Saturday morning. Lent had run its course. I felt the depressing effect of Holy Week and Good Friday services; the apparent triumph of evil over good, money, betrayal, desertion; power, political ploys, a trial with justice expedient and truth irrelevant. I was profoundly depressed; not in a clinical sense but simply as a result of the way the Church bathed her feet in the events leading up to the crucifixion. Did anyone really need to be reminded to this extent of the way we are? I looked forward to the liturgy of Easter morning, with its joy and hope to spur me to go on; to work at those parts of my job about which I was convinced.

Although she didn't say so I had no doubt that Jennifer looked forward to Easter, but for her own reasons. In a confused sort of way I was looking forward to Easter for her reasons too, since, believe it or not, she was easier to live with when she was drinking than when she wasn't. As Lent progressed she became more irritable and argumentative.

'Will you for God's sake say something?' She spat across the table, breaking the silence between us. 'You're sitting there with a face like the Scotsman who lost a sixpence and found a threepenny bit.' I chose not to reply but continued to look out the window into the garden that was burgeoning with the impulse of spring. In the lawn daffodils still bloomed in their planned asymmetry and crocuses under the beech tree at the end were a mist of purple and orange. Everywhere colour and the fresh green of new growth mocked my state of mind.

'I'm sorry,' I said. 'I know I'm bad company.'

'What's wrong?' she asked.

'The usual, I don't know whether I should be in this job at all or not.'

Ever since I was a child I had had more questions than answers about the Christian faith. When I aired my questions my elders and betters never seemed to take them seriously. They either ignored them or gave me answers that didn't address my questions, in such a way that I knew there was no point in pursuing the matter. I often felt foolish that something that was a problem to me didn't seem to be a problem to anybody I broached it with. When I entered divinity school the more I learned the more questions I had, but I didn't get satisfaction there either. I was met by my peers with anything from pity to impatience, and those whose responsibility it was to teach, with odd exceptions, weren't much help. Occasionally someone came over onto my ground as a device to mollify me; on more than one occasion as a way to avoid answering the question I was told that doubt was the natural corollary of faith. I got on with my life and kept my doubts to myself apart from the occasional discussion with Jennifer. According to her there was more than enough work with parishioners to keep me busy without indulging the luxury of a struggle with belief.

'You've weathered it all before,' Jennifer said, 'and our break at Mary's after Easter will do you good. Time away from the parish will cheer you up. At the end of the day it's family that makes it all worthwhile.' I knew that Jennifer believed what she said about the importance of family, but these days opportunities to drink seemed for her to take precedence over everything else.

'I may not be able to go if Fred is about to expire.'

'Of course you can, he might struggle on for weeks, and anyway you can come back if he dies.' Jennifer no longer went to church. For years her attendance had been sporadic, but for some time now she had stopped altogether. She took the bits of Christianity that made sense to her and ignored the rest, but she understood why it wasn't so easy for me to do the same. 'If it all becomes too much for you, you can chuck it up and we can move to the city where I can teach.'

'And what would I do?' I asked. 'I'm trained for nothing else.'

'If you decide you can't stay that's something you'll have to face. Something'll turn up.'

'The question is can I stay on my own terms? Who draws the line?'

We had come to this point many times before. Sometimes the demands of the job dulled my conscience and caused me to put it all to the back of my mind. At other times my conscience gave me great unease, particularly when I had to put together some ideas for a sermon. Who was I to preach to others? How far was I to give the party line and how far could I raise questions of my own? My instinct was to get people to move on in their faith by asking questions rather than encouraging them to swallow it all hook line and sinker.

Jennifer went upstairs to dress. I washed up the few dishes in the sink and went down to the church where the usual women were decorating for Easter. It's what clergy call 'putting in an appearance;' a device to encourage parish workers in whatever it is they are doing to keep them happy. Some of them think that what they do in the parish they do for the clergy personally and if the rector doesn't see them on the job and give them a pat on the back parishioners may lose heart or even take the huff.

Decorating the church was as important a ritual as Easter itself. All the women had their own allotted areas of the church on which to display their talents. This was when the flower club ladies came into their own. There were, however, some non-flower club women who had a different approach; they preferred less formal arrangements using grasses and leaves that displayed nature's talents rather than set pieces with blooms that displayed how able the arranger was. Responsibility for some of the areas of the church for decoration had been passed down in families, and some of the younger women were no more than 'hewers of wood and drawers of water' for their mothers or mothers-in-law. I wandered around the church, chatted to the women and made all the usual noises to give the necessary approval to all their efforts and then went down the village for the paper.

After lunch I took a phone call in the study from one of the decorators. I went to the kitchen to recount the inevitable to Jennifer, primarily because she would help me to keep my patience.

'Mrs Bowers didn't turn up to decorate the baptistry and none of the others dared touch it.'

'Maybe she's sick,' Jennifer said charitably.

'She's sick all right,' I said, 'but not in the way you mean. Sylvia met her in the village after they had all finished and she said she wouldn't be decorating this year. I bet Bob has finally lost patience with her. I've a good mind to leave her bit of the church untouched and tell anyone who asks, exactly why.' I knew well I wouldn't, but I felt like it. 'She's a cantankerous temperamental old bitch, but I'll have to phone her to try to give her a way back.'

Mrs Bowers confirmed frostily that she would not be decorating the baptistry this year, and proceeded to give me the whole convoluted story about Bob, the keys and the flower jars. I remained neutral and listened to her talking but made no effort to follow the details. If she had stayed away because she had difficulty with the resurrection I'd have understood, but not because of a bunch of keys and a few flower jars. It reminded me how, in some ways, I was poles apart from some of my parishioners and yet I had a responsibility to love them all wherever they were at; an almost impossible job.

'Come on,' said Jennifer, 'we'd better do it, nobody else will,' and we cut some things in the garden and went down to the church. Even we felt we were treading on holy ground decorating the baptistery that only Mrs Bowers had done in living memory.

The early communion of Easter morning worked its magic. The greeting 'Christ is risen,' the Gloria again after Lent, no sermon and the gospel writer's utter conviction in recounting the events of the first Easter morning; the astonishment of the disciples and the empty tomb. When our daughter Mary was a teenager she used to say: 'Chill out Dad, and go with the flow.' I did that morning and it worked. I stopped my head working and listened to my heart. I had a great sense of peace and hope. There were spring festivals and rituals of new life and hope long before Christianity, but Easter was the spring festival of my tribe and the high point of the Christian year. I hoped that Jennifer, who occasionally went to church at Christmas or Easter, might experience something of the same peace and hope that I did.

That Easter morning didn't remove my questions about the resurrection, but it made them irrelevant for the moment. At no other time of year did I wonder more about what people actually believed, and I marvelled at how little I knew about what they did believe. I knew what I believed myself and it made sense to me, but what did parishioners make of it all? I often felt like asking one of them.

'Tell me, what do you make of the resurrection?' I wouldn't, of course, put anyone on the spot like that, but I would like to have known. Nobody ever volunteered this kind of information. It wasn't the ones who bought the package and didn't want to know what was inside it that worried me, they all seemed to be happy with themselves. It was the few who did want to look inside the package and found it incredible, that I wanted to hear.

It wasn't long before I was brought back to earth. Jennifer went out that night and, tired after the day, I went early to bed. I woke in the morning to the strong smell of stale alcohol, which I hadn't had for the whole of Lent. Jennifer lay on her side facing me half covered; she was out to the world. I dismissed the naive hope I had had that she might stay off drink or even that she might have one or two and come home early. I thought, as I often did, how so many people could enjoy a couple of drinks and leave it at that. I pulled the bedclothes over her and she didn't stir. Her greying unkempt hair was strealed across the pillow and her freckled skin was taut across her cheekbones. I don't believe she ever went to the hairdresser other than for a cut. She used only clasps and combs, from which wisps always escaped that seemed to symbolise her disregard for what other people might think. Propped up on my elbow I watched her breathing and remembered how feminine she had been when we married even though lipstick and a little perfume were the only cosmetics she had used.

When we were married Jennifer had said to me: 'You know I'm not very religious, but I'll do whatever I can to help you.' Above all else she had been honest and had been true to her word and supported me. She liked people and she was kind. She put people at their ease when they called to the rectory, and she went to meetings she had no interest in. She was loyal but never shy of telling me when she thought I was wrong. In addition she made friends, inside and outside the parish, and had a life of her own. As I watched her I thought how in recent times we had grown apart; it was ages since we had had a proper heart-to-heart and when I tried, it usually ended with angry words. She didn't see her friends these days either.

I got up and went down to the kitchen in my dressing-gown. The electric kettle had boiled dry: the safety device had pushed the plug out. Jennifer had plugged it in, probably sat down and fallen asleep, had woken, couldn't fix it, and went to bed. I dreaded the beginning of another cycle of concealment, denial and silence. I was helpless to do anything but stand by and watch things getting worse for both of us. I knew enough about the problem to know that denial was at its centre: Jennifer's denial that there was a problem at all.

'I can't understand how you can be so stupid as to think I have a problem when I can stop drinking whenever I want.' I wasn't so stupid as not to know that when she was dry for a while a batter, during which she would be completely out of control, was not far away.

I sat into the chair beside the cooker and tried to poke the safety pin back into the kettle. I was on holiday and had no parish responsibilities. In my mind I built an imaginary wall around the rectory to protect me from the demands of parishioners. The house, which was normally open house, was now private, and I wanted to stay safely inside, and although I couldn't, I felt like leaving the phone off the hook. The trouble was the parishioners were not aware that there was a wall around the rectory with a 'private' sign on top. I fixed the kettle, filled it and plugged it in. I made tea and brought a cup upstairs to Jennifer. She was still asleep; she hadn't moved. I sat in the kitchen and drank tea wondering how long Jennifer could go on drinking without damaging her health. Recently she looked wretched and only picked at her food.

The phone rang in the hall. I swore and was tempted not to answer it, when I remembered it might be Mary to find out when to expect us.

'Hello.'

'This is Michael Leonard. Daddy's dead.'

'Michael, I'm sorry. When?'

'About half an hour ago.'

'I'll be out right away.'

'Thank you.'

I put down the phone and sat with my hand still on the receiver. I felt a great sadness, for I was five years older than Fred and he hadn't lived to see grandchildren. I went upstairs, washed and dressed and put on my clericals. I shook Jennifer.

'Fred died half an hour ago. I'm going out there now.'

'Oh, oh,' she muttered but didn't fully come round and when I was at the door she said:

'What?'

'Fred Leonard is dead.' It took a second to sink in.

'Poor Vera.' She said, and sank back on the pillow.

I drove slowly, reminding myself not to say the trite things that have no meaning. Vera had spoken bravely of Fred's death recently, but now it would be different. He was dead, and it would most likely be, in the short term, a relief; what a dozen people will say to her over the next few days: 'It's a happy release.' It is and it isn't.

As I drove into the yard I reminded myself how important the presence of clergy is to people at a time of death. I always felt that responsibility. Someone had recently moved the bar on the silage pit as I could hear the sound of the cattle munching at the face. There were only family cars in the yard. I pushed in the back door; there was nobody in the kitchen. I found Michael and Vera in the sitting-room making a list. Carol was on her way from Dublin; she had been down to see her father the previous day. Vera told me what happened; Fred had died suddenly in the end. She was beyond tears. Bernie was upstairs with a neighbour helping to lay Fred out.

Michael asked when the funeral should be. We arranged the day and time and drafted a notice for the paper. Michael and Vera chose hymns; the hackneyed old favourites for funerals, 'Abide with me,' 'Rock of Ages' and 'Shall We Gather at the River?' These hymns indulged the assurance that despite the tragedy of death there was somebody in charge and something better to come, and despite the fact I didn't believe this myself I was always happy for people to have these hymns at funerals if they were a comfort to them. After all isn't that what religion is for? It was important for the family to do things according to local custom, not to be different so as not to give people cause to gossip.

Bernie came downstairs to say they were finished. We all went up to the room that had been cleared of all the accoutrements of sickness and dying. The mirrors on the dressing table and wardrobe had been draped with sheets. I looked at Fred, covered to the chin with a white sheet, to confirm the stillness of death. There could be pain only while there was life. Death was preferable to what Fred had endured for the last few months, and even if the vicious rumour that there was a hell were true I was as sure as I was alive that Fred would not end up there. I didn't think it unreasonable that other people should believe or hope that physical death was not the end. I did not expect others to believe as I did.

We stood around the bed, Michael with one arm around his mother and the other round his wife carrying Fred's unborn grandchild. I had no idea what might be going through their minds

– happy memories, regrets, wondering what next, the assurance of heaven or some trivial or mundane detail about the next couple of days. I said some prayers, mainly of thanksgiving for Fred's life and what he meant to those who loved him as a husband and father. When my own beliefs didn't square with the prayers of the Church I believed my beliefs were irrelevant since I was acting, not in a personal capacity but for the Church on behalf of the community.

We went down to the kitchen and drank tea. The undertaker, who had buried Fred's parents and whose father had buried Fred's grandparents, arrived. I confirmed the times with him and left the family to work out the final details of the death notice for the paper.

In the rectory kitchen Jennifer sat beside the cooker in her dressing-gown, with a mug of coffee. She looked wretched.

'How is Vera?' she asked.

'Worn out.'

'Is Carol there?'

'No, she's on her way. You were late last night.'

Jennifer didn't reply.

'Why don't you stay off drink altogether? It's undermining your health and it costs money. If you stopped we could have a decent holiday. We could go to Florence to see the things you've always talked about.'

'I only drink for company. It's lonely here on my own if I don't go out.'

The truth was that I knew Jennifer had a drink problem. I hadn't yet said it to her in so many words and decided now was the time. There was no easy way to say it, so I came straight out with it:

'Jennifer, you have a serious drink problem,' I said. I couldn't bring myself to use the word 'alcoholic,' as she had always been such an individual I couldn't label her in that way, but if I'm honest I didn't use the word for fear she would become angry and it wasn't the moment for that.

'How, in God's name, if you still believe in him, can you say I have a drink problem when I spent the last six weeks without a drink?'

'You say you can give it up when you like. Maybe you can, but you can't give up going back on it, and when you're drinking you can't give up drinking too much.' Now having gone so far I felt I might as well be hanged for a sheep as a lamb: 'Will you please me and go to Alcoholics Anonymous, and if they say you don't need help I'll accept it.'

I could see a sudden surge of anger which Jennifer stifled, and in as controlled a way as she could she said: 'Yes, I will ….sometime.' Anger would have filled her own need, but a measured response was a more effective way to stave me off. She put her mug on the drain-board and went upstairs.

CHAPTER 5

I had no great hope that Jennifer would go to AA. She was too much her own person and if she decided to stop drinking she would feel she didn't need help from anyone. She was strong willed and if she came to the conclusion she should stop, I believed there was a fair chance she could do it on her own.

My thoughts returned to Fred, who never took more than an odd glass of sherry or bottle of beer on special occasions. Was there a reason for everything? Fred probably died of lung cancer because he smoked, but not everyone who smokes dies of lung cancer. Why was Jennifer an alcoholic? Not everyone who drinks becomes an alcoholic. What about childhood deaths, accidents, epidemics, diseases, wars? My mind raced on and on over all the topics that showed the incompatibility of pain and suffering in the world with the existence of an all-powerful and all-loving God. I had gone over this kind of thing a thousand times before and had come to the conclusion that life is like being dealt a hand of cards, and living is how well we play them. Some people are dealt a terrible hand, and some a good one; and some people whatever cards they get play them badly and others play theirs well.

At around midday I went back to Leonards. Michael met me in the yard. He was shy and I had never really come to know him. After we said 'hello' he talked about his father, and suddenly said:

'Where is he now?' He asked the question in such a disarming way that he seemed to expect a simple answer. I resisted the temptation to give him a lot of theological claptrap, which was inconclusive anyway about whether the Church believed people went straight to heaven or hell or were somewhere in suspense waiting for a last judgement, or some combination of these. I could never disentangle the whole thing myself and it wasn't something I found important. In the circumstances I felt responsible to tell him what the Church taught, rather than what I believed myself, but then I wasn't sure what the Church did teach.

'To be honest I don't know what the Church says, other than it believes in some form of life after death. Myself, I simply have no idea, but if there is life after death I don't believe it has to do with reward and punishment.' Michael listened carefully and said:

'Thank you.'

As we turned towards the back door he said: 'I'm not sure, what to believe, but I don't think there is life after death.' He opened the door, stood back and let me in ahead of him.

People in the farming community do what they can in a practical way at a time of death. Women bake cakes and make sandwiches, and men dig the grave, help with the milking or look after the stock. Neighbours and friends had taken over Leonards' kitchen and were doing what needed to be done. One of the women informed me:

'Rector, the fire is lighting in the sitting-room,' the suitable place for a rector in the circumstances. Soon there would be a steady stream of callers and all of them would be asked: 'Would you like to go up to the room?' and all would go to view the corpse and make what re-assuring comments they could. Some would say predictable and even foolish things, other would say little and a few would not say anything but put a sympathetic hand on Vera's shoulder or arm. In the presence of death all would want to help and all would feel inadequate.

I went to the sitting-room, where I found Vera tidying things away and arranging chairs. We sat beside the fire and one of the neighbours brought a tray with tea, sandwiches and some huge wedges of sponge cake. For me it was important simply to be available. Vera broke the silence between us:

'Coming away from the churchyard at his mother's funeral, Fred said to me: "We'll be the next generation into the ground." Little did he know how soon it would be,' and not waiting for a response she continued; 'Carol is on her way, she should be here any time now; she and her Dad were close.' I made a trite comment about fathers and daughters and then Michael came in to say somebody had arrived and Vera left to meet them. I finished my tea and went out to the kitchen where I spoke to the helpers and then Michael came out to the yard to see me off.

When I arrived home Jennifer told me that Mr Armstrong had phoned.

'What did he want?'

'He wanted to know how the plans for the anniversary of the church were going.'

'That's all I need. What did you tell him?'

'I told him you were out with a family arranging a funeral, and in fact you were on holiday this week and would he phone you sometime next week.'

'What did he say?'

'He said, "Thank you" and put down the phone. The stupid man.'

'You should have used the vernacular and told him to fuck off.'

Jennifer was always protective of me from the unreasonable demands of parishioners. She thought I was too soft and she would let them know gently but firmly if she thought they were inconsiderate.

On the day of the funeral I arrived at the front of the house which, though seldom used, was opened up for the occasion. The avenue from the front gate had been edged, the gravel scuffled and some of the overgrown shrubs cut back. Neighbours, mostly men in their Sunday suits, stood around in groups outside talking, and the hearse with wreaths on top was parked beside the steps. I spoke briefly to the undertaker to be assured all was in order and went up the steps into the hall that was full of people talking quietly. They parted like the Red Sea to let me through the hall and sitting-room to where the family stood on one side of the open coffin, Vera between Carol and Michael. I wondered what all these people thought as they looked at the waxen emaciated face. I thought of Michael's question, 'Where is he now?' and wondered if they all had the same question or whether they thought they knew or thought about it at all.

I spoke to Vera to be sure she was ready and then standing at the head of the coffin I began the prayers. I was never sure to what extent prayers at funerals were simply part of the ritual as a comfort for people or were addressed to God in the hope of being answered. I was always careful not to use a prayer in the church that I had already said at the house. I could imagine God saying 'The silly fool, he asked me that half an hour ago.' However, I was inclined to believe that the funeral service was primarily designed to express the feelings of the family at the time of death and to reassure them. When I finished I said to Vera:

'Come in your own time,' and as I turned to look at the corpse for a second I thought, 'God love you, Fred,' without really knowing what I meant; it was simply my way of saying goodbye. As I turned for the door the Red Sea parted again to let me out.

A large crowd of people stood in groups outside the church, and there was a handful of people inside. I robed and when the funeral arrived I met the coffin at the gate and led it into the church. Despite the numbers, some pews at the front opposite the family remained empty while people stood at the back and overflowed into the porch and outside.

The service reminded God of his promises: 'I am the resurrection and the life, saith the Lord: he that believes in me, though he were dead, yet shall he live: and whosoever lives and believes in me shall never die…The Lord is my shepherd, I shall not want….Now Christ is risen from the dead and become the first fruits of them that slept …. But some man will say, how are the dead raised up ? Thou fool …. Sown in corruption….raised in incorruption. … sown in dishonour, raised in glory …flesh and blood cannot inherit the kingdom of God… Behold I shew you a mystery….O death, where is thy sting? O grave, where is thy victory?' The reassuring prayers and the emotion-laden hymns, and then to the churchyard: the coffin lowered into the plastic grass-lined grave and the words of committal, 'earth to earth, ashes to ashes, dust to dust' to the hum of gossip from the outer reaches of the crowd.

Back at the house; tea, sandwiches and cakes, and relations that only meet at weddings and funerals, friends and neighbours doing all they can do, the women serving and the men being served. Relaxed conversation about anything under the sun, reflecting the deep down relief that the burial is over and things are on their way back to normal, for everyone except Vera and the family who, when they all drift away, are left to face the void.

I was angry that old Armstrong had phoned about the church anniversary. I grant him that he had left it until after the busyness of Easter to phone, not knowing that if it weren't for Fred's funeral I would be on holiday. People who don't have a regular job think that people who work are as free as they are and, of course, people who have a regular job think that people who don't work have nothing to do all day.

I simply had no interest in an anniversary celebration, but I knew I had to organise something because, as Jennifer kept telling me, it would be good for the parish, good for the whole community and it would be fun. It wasn't my idea of fun, but Robert Armstrong's gift of money made it imperative that I do something. I was clear in my own mind that he wanted an event to celebrate the place of his family in the history of the parish and the area. The God whom he wanted to celebrate was a God he made much in his own image. A God, however, who had placed him at the end of his line, just about surviving and hanging on to whatever he could of the past. Some parishioners would see it as an occasion to affirm their distinctive tradition. Though small in number, they believed their tradition was high in quality and they would be glad to have an excuse to display it to their Catholic friends and neighbours. For some parishioners their only distinctiveness in the community was that they were Protestant. Others would value the opportunity to return something of the goodwill and support the majority tribe gave to the minority tribe by involving as many of them as possible.

A few would resent this and want the event to affirm their Protestant exclusiveness. I had no stomach for getting into this minefield but had to do something.

I talked to Jennifer about it; she knew how much I dreaded the whole idea.

'You're as dull as ditchwater,' she said, 'you're a spoilsport, a killjoy. What is there in life if you can't have the odd celebration? You must let your hair down from time to time before it's too late and you have none left to let down.'

I knew that I was the problem. I had great difficulty running this kind of event, and I used to defend myself by saying there was nothing in the ordination service or the institution service to a parish about being an entertainments officer. This event would be a bit different from the usual parish social event and I knew the parishioners would do most of the work, but I would have a responsibility for the whole thing.

Jennifer told me: 'It says nothing in the ordination service about many things you do without complaint. You do them because you enjoy doing them, or they give you some kind of satisfaction, and for some strange reason there's nothing for you in this kind of thing.'

Of course she was right, so I would have to press ahead despite not enjoying it one bit and then, as she so often did, she summed it up succinctly:

'The trouble with you is you have no interest in religion, only in theology.'

'That's not entirely true. I'm interested in religion that comes from a thought-out theology. So much of what we do is folk religion that barely tips its hat to Christianity.'

This all sounded more pompous and self-righteous than I intended, but Jennifer knew what I meant as we had been there many times before. I enjoyed these discussions with her; she had a sharper mind than I had, if a little less well-informed on this topic. She also kept herself detached: I was too involved and I was always glad of her perspective, while not always agreeing with it. In her own way she had more of a religious sense than I had. She saw the Church as providing formal worship, available to people when they wanted it, and some wanted it every week or even every day, while others wanted it only from time to time. She saw no reason for going every Sunday as a discipline, out of habit or in order not to let the side down.

'The only reason that clergy expect people to turn up every Sunday,' she would say, 'is because when they lay on a service they feel let down if lots of people don't attend. They take it as a personal slight when people don't come. Clergy have to be there, but parishioners have a choice. Furthermore if people don't attend regularly there would be less money on the plate and the whole thing would collapse. This kind of religion is collapsing anyway, and maybe it's no harm. Something better will emerge that will express what people want to say and the whole shebang that we're struggling to keep going will go, and let's hope you get your pension before it does.'

I listened and in my own mind filled in things she often said.

'The Church is obsessed with numbers and money.' It was hard to argue with that. 'How can it be right for everyone to go to church every Sunday?' she would say. 'People are different; going every Sunday is part of the Church's need to control people rather than to meet their needs.'

'You're always telling me that buildings are not important,' I goaded her, 'and now you want me to create a great fuss because one of them happens to be there for a hundred and fifty years.'

'God give me patience; you're trying to provoke me,' she said raising her hands in the air, 'The church and the hundred and fifty years are only an excuse. What's wrong with you? You're so bloody intense about it.'

I didn't get away for my post-Easter break, but took the rest of the week off as far as that is possible while living in a rectory. You can't tell people who phone or call to the door: 'I'm on holiday: try again next week.' Jennifer would like to have done that, simply as a matter of justice as she was the only one who knew all the aspects of the job and how hard I worked. Parishioners tended to understand my work only insofar as it affected them.

I confronted the inevitable and on the following Sunday I announced a meeting to plan the celebrations for the one hundred and fiftieth anniversary of the church. I preached a sermon without conviction about two things; the value of Christian witness and the place of tradition in the life of the Church. I did it not because I was convinced by either of these concepts, but because they were the two reasons most people would feel were valid reasons for having a celebration. In fact self-conscious Christian witness seemed to me to be arrogant and often based on pride, while tradition, having some value as a teacher was, more often than not, a tyrant. I didn't want to influence other people to my point of view but wanted to try to be fair to everyone who might be happy to go along with a festival or even, like Jennifer, to be enthusiastic about one.

CHAPTER 6

Siobhán Stacey did not make her First Holy Communion, and started in her new school after Easter. I never did know exactly why Kate wanted Siobhán to make the change. Either she didn't want her in the school where she taught or she wanted a smaller school with a better pupil/teacher ratio and a more liberal regime. Maybe she didn't want Siobhán to be tagged with what her Dad had done, or perhaps it was a combination of some or all of these. If Jennifer was in the village after school time she would call to see Kate, who had plenty of local chat. Jennifer denied that it was gossip, but rather news that made her feel part of the broader community.

I was making no progress with Jennifer about her drinking. She was back to her old routine and wouldn't brook any discussion of it. Apart altogether from the money and what people thought, neither of which was of great concern to me, Jennifer saw my disapproval of her drinking in almost everything I said, and this was driving us further apart. Though I was not concerned about what people thought, I had a sense from some parishioners that they were sympathetic and from others that they were censorious.

I decided to call to Kate one afternoon I knew Jennifer would not be there. Kate lived in a house that she and Conor had built when they were married. Conor, an architect, had given free rein to his creativity and had built a house that was for a while the wonder of the village. It was off the end of the village street up Rafter's Lane that led to a derelict farmhouse. You came upon it round a bend on the lane that was lined with mature beech and to my mind this modern man-made construction screamed at its pastoral setting. Kate had tried to get Conor to buy the derelict early nineteenth century farmhouse and renovate it, but he couldn't resist the opportunity to try for himself something that was too adventurous for his clients.

Conor and Betty had moved to the city since they disappeared together. Betty was the only daughter of a prominent parishioner family with a large farm. She was a capable and progressive farmer who had been running the family farm and living with her parents. She was the kind of woman that everybody assumed, if she ever married, it would be to a farmer. Her father had not given up hope that she would eventually find the city and Conor no longer tolerable, and come home. If she did and if he had his way not a word, of what he considered an aberration, would be mentioned and she could take up where she left off. He was certain, however, that he would not have his way, since his wife was a different kettle of fish, being much more unforgiving.

Betty's mother had come from a cottage on the side of the road and had married into an old farming family with a fine house and a substantial farm. She was a determined woman and from the beginning she was conscious of her improved social status and everything she did was calculated to maintain, if not to enhance, it. She laboured, however, under the misapprehension that the family's status in the community was based solely on their possession of money and land, and she judged everything by monetary and material criteria. Initially she was incredulous that her daughter would run away with a married man and a Catholic to boot, but her incredulity did not last long. She came out fighting and called to see Kate demanding to know Betty's whereabouts. Kate, herself distraught at the time, didn't invite her in, told her politely she didn't know and closed the door. Betty's mother phoned twice after that and Kate asked her not to phone again.

Betty's mother wasn't used to not getting her own way. When crossed she was bitter, and she was determined that whatever transpired Betty would be punished for the disgrace she had brought on the family, and she was also determined that she had forfeited her right to the farm. Her mother expected to survive her husband, who was more than ten years older than she was and from whom she had arranged that she alone would inherit. She had already alienated Betty's only sibling, a younger brother, who had made it clear that he had no interest in farming and had made a life for himself in Dublin.

Knowing her mother's bitter intransigence, Betty had not been back since she left, and she had been in touch only a couple of times with her parents, and then only through her brother. She knew her father would be loyal to her mother, since to have been otherwise would have made life intolerable for him. Because her mother had spoken unforgiving words, she would not budge an inch even if Betty were to repent and prostrate herself on the ground before her. Not only had Betty disgraced the family, she had disgraced the tribe, and her mother's intransigence was her way of saying; 'she's no part of us and as far as we're concerned she's as good as dead.'

For Betty's mother, Jennifer's friendship with Kate would have made Jennifer one of "the enemy," and I have no doubt she had said something like: 'What else would you expect from a rector's wife that frequents a public house in the village?' Though she said nothing to me, I'm sure that I was, by association, implicated in the treachery too.

I turned off the lane into the entrance to the house and up the curved avenue through the live-and-let-live front garden to the hall door where Siobhán was playing on the step. She was no longer shy with me since she saw me going in and out of school:

'I'm brushing my doll's hair.'

I sat on the step while she showed me her dolls and I was the shy one when she showed me what they were wearing, down to the last stitch. I took my leave of Siobhán, rang the bell and through a delightful aroma wafting through the hall, I found Kate in her designer kitchen clearing up after baking. As always she gave me a warm welcome, washed her hands and put on the kettle.

'I'll just finish up here and then I can relax.'

Kate smiled readily and had the happy knack of putting people at their ease, and above all she was gentle. The more I came to know her the harder I found it to understand how Conor could have left her.

'I'm sure Jennifer has told you how happy Siobhán is at school,' she said, 'and it has taken a load off my mind, not least because she would have been in my class next year.'

'I'm glad it has worked out so well. She introduced me to all her dolls on the step.'

'I worry that she misses her Dad. Not only did Conor abandon me, he abandoned Siobhán and whatever I'm supposed to have done, Siobhán certainly didn't do anything to deserve it. How could he?'

'As I've told you before, it's a mystery to me how he could have abandoned either of you. Now tell me about you.'

'I'm doing fine. If you had told me two years ago I would be doing so well at this stage I wouldn't have believed you.'

'Kate, you're marvellous.'

She filled up and turned away to wipe down the drain board.

'I've really come about Jennifer and her drinking. Whatever I say doesn't make a blind bit of difference, and it's become a no-go area between us.'

'I know, I've wondered about it myself,' Kate said, 'but I didn't think it was that bad. I occasionally go with her to Foley's, but I leave early as my baby-sitter has to be home by ten.'

Kate finished what she was doing, tidied her baking things into the sink and ran the tap on them. She made two mugs of coffee, put one in front of me and sat on the opposite side of the counter.

'It's worse than you realise; she comes home most nights in the small hours the worse for wear. You know how much she cares for you and admires you; perhaps you could talk to her. If she'll listen to anybody she'll listen to you. Don't say I asked; that'll be a red rag to a bull, and an excuse not to listen, but if you say you've noticed she might give you a hearing, but I'm not hopeful even of that. I think she needs professional help, but you know what they say: it doesn't matter what anyone else thinks, drinkers have to want to stop themselves.'

As I said all this I realised there was no point in Kate saying anything to Jennifer. It would be better if she didn't, as Jennifer might turn against her if she appeared to come between her and her drink, and she would need Kate's love and care later on.

'On second thoughts, Kate, maybe it's better if you don't say anything. She'll know I put you up to it and it'll only make things worse, but it's good to talk to you about it. There's nobody else I can talk to, and particularly I don't want to worry the children.'

'I don't mind talking to Jennifer about her drinking; she talked to me recently about having given it up for Lent, and how she'd hate it to get hold of her so that she couldn't stop.'

'She can give it up for Lent all right, but she can't stop. I've no idea what parishioners think or people in the village, and I don't really care, but there must be talk. The hard thing is that I feel completely helpless as I see her getting worse, and the hardest thing of all is that I have lost touch with her. She has erected a barrier between us, behind which she lives a life of her own in which she brooks no interference. My hope is that she won't damage her health irreparably before she gets help. I don't want to lose her.'

My voice cracked slightly and it was my turn for tears to well up, but they didn't break. I took out my handkerchief and blew my nose. Kate put her hand gently on mine and said:

'I know what you mean.'

'Of course you do,' I said, 'I shouldn't be burdening you with my problems.'

I stood up. 'I'd better be off. Thank you for listening.'

Kate came to the door where Siobhán was still playing on the step.

'This one has no coat; Mummy is going to make one when she gets time.'

When I got to the gate I looked in the rear view mirror. Kate was waving with Siobhán in her arms hugging Kate tightly around the neck.

As I drove through the village I saw two cars parked outside the church. I recognised one of them and stopped and went in. Robert Armstrong and a painter I didn't know, in overalls, were standing in the sanctuary looking up at the back of the chancel arch. When they saw me Mr Armstrong came down the aisle.

'Ah, rector, I'm deciding what has to be done.' I felt a surge of annoyance verging on anger, but said nothing. 'It's quite a job, but the whole church needs to be painted; if we only do one part it will scream at the rest. Do you think we could get away without varnishing the beams?'

I couldn't avoid the direct question, but didn't want to be drawn into his presumption and interference.

'I don't know,' I said curtly. I resented that he was pushing me to get on with something in which I had no interest. I also resented the fact that this was the only thing in the parish in which he had taken an interest since I came. 'We'll have to get the churchwardens to see what needs to be done and make a recommendation to the vestry. They will decide,' I added, resorting, as I didn't often do, to the correct procedure in such matters. He knew enough to know he could not challenge that, and called the painter down the aisle. He introduced the painter to me and then asked his opinion on the beams.

I walked away to detach myself from their discussion. I wanted to wait to speak to Robert Armstrong on his own to tell him that despite the fact that he was paying for it, he would have to leave it to the vestry and that I would ensure the job was done and done well. I stood and looked at the stained glass east window and realised I had never looked at it closely before. It was a figure of Jesus holding a crook, a lamb in his other arm and some sheep behind him. At the bottom was a text: 'I am the Good Shepherd.'

My irritation abated slowly as I became absorbed in the window. It was not the subject that caught my imagination, but the beauty of the work. I imagined the artist with pencil and paper starting to sketch. I knew nothing of the process, but wondered how he decided on the size and shape of each piece. I imagined a workshop with benches covered with pieces of coloured glass and strips of lead, and perhaps an apprentice working away at one small corner unable to visualise the whole. The dedication underneath the window read: "In memory of Alicia Armstrong, only daughter of Robert and Jane Armstrong, died 14th January 1832, aged 23 years." It could have been an accident, a burst appendix or almost anything; if it had been a hunting accident they would have said so. The window was badly buckled in places and needed attention. It would have suited the current Armstrong better to have the window repaired than to interfere in the decoration.

I moved away and read the inscription on a tablet in the choir: "To the memory of Capt. John Armstrong who died, 18th December 1815, of wounds received at Waterloo." There were some wall tablets with coats-of-arms of other families – all important people long since forgotten.

Changed times. Robert Armstrong struggled to survive in his ancestral home. It was a great pity he couldn't keep the house in reasonable repair. It was part of the heritage of the area. His ancestors had been top of the heap because in their day they were able soldiers, administrators and diplomats. Robert himself had a good history degree from Cambridge, he had spent two years in Africa and had come home and tried to farm the small amount of land that remained. Socially he behaved as if nothing had changed in the past hundred years; I once heard him talking about his father's burial in the family tomb surrounded in the churchyard by his tenants. He was living in an unreal world of his family's former status. Blood was everything; it was inconceivable that he would marry outside his class, which probably accounted for his bachelor condition and apparently was more important than the onus he must have felt to provide an heir. I did suspect, however, that there might be another reason. As Irish society evolved he was paying the price for his reluctance to adapt. He was not surviving. Rather he was grasping at straws, such as the hundred and fiftieth anniversary of the church, to affirm the status the Armstrongs no longer had.

The families in the village were in the ascendant and the Armstrong family was in decline. Education and economic prosperity had made for a confident middle-class that was getting on with life in business and the professions, and for whom 'the big house' was an irrelevance. Robert Armstrong's view of the world and theirs were poles apart. He had all the time in the world, which he used to try to turn back the clock or at least to slow it down. The people of the village were too busy to give the clock more than an occasional cursory glance. Robert had become something of a curiosity, and his odd ways were the cause of mild amusement in the village. In his infrequent dealings with local people they were indulgent of his old world manner and the polite distance he kept, and they treated him largely with benign indifference. The only business his family had conducted locally for many years was with the undertaker.

'We think the beams should be varnished.' The voice startled me. The royal 'we,' or he and the painter I wasn't sure.

'If you include it with what you would like to see done, I will put your ideas to the vestry,' I said.

He went back to the painter who made a note in his book as if he had the job in the bag. I left the church and went out into the warm early summer afternoon. The churchyard would need a thorough restoration before this festival, but no doubt the parishioners would save money by doing it themselves.

I couldn't face going home. Jennifer's lies and lame excuses for going out disturbed me. Before her whole personality had become subsumed by her need for alcohol she was direct and honest. Now she was devious and untruthful, and I found it hard to take. Such was my distress about the chaos of Jennifer's drinking that the good times of the past had faded from memory, or even disappeared altogether. I had to make a special effort to recall happier days, or perhaps a photograph would be a reminder of the fun Jennifer had with the children when they were small or her youthful empathy with them in the struggles of their teenage years. When they came home now there was great joy, but they seemed to come in from outside, from a world of their own. They seemed removed and not from a shared past, and this added to the poignancy of my isolation from Jennifer and the tyranny of her drinking.

I sat into the car and became aware of how defeated I felt on all fronts. Over the years I had learned that when I was low, two things could lift my spirits. One I had done earlier in the afternoon; visit somebody I knew would be glad to see me, Kate, and I felt the better for having done that. The other was to make a visit I dreaded, and then feel virtuous for having done it. I started the car and drove out the far side of the village into the country.

Bill and Kathleen were long overdue a visit. They were both in their late fifties and lived in a cottage that went with Bill's job as a farm labourer. Their only child, a daughter, was married and living in England. I dreaded going to see them; they had an inflated view of clergy: with them respectability was everything and a pastoral visit was a big event. I had the impression that when they spoke they were always fearful of saying something wrong, something I might not approve of, and this made conversation stilted and difficult. They would have known of Jennifer's drinking, and as parishioners they would have been scandalized by it, largely because it would have reflected on them badly because of what their Catholic neighbours would think.

Bill was a small spare man with a shock of grey hair and a ruddy complexion. He always wore a suit – the same threadbare one for as long as I had known him. Never in my hearing did he ever speak to his wife, and it wouldn't have surprised me if he never did. The only piece of conversation Bill would initiate was to make a comment on the weather and having done that he would then respond to anything I said by repeating the key words.

'Well, Bill, it was a great harvest this year.'

'A great harvest.'

'The price of cattle has gone through the roof.'

'Through the roof.'

If I asked a simple question he would answer it with either 'yes, yes, yes,' or 'no, no, no.' If the answer was not just a matter of fact, but implied an opinion, he would precede his trinity of 'yes's' or 'no's' with 'Oh,' for emphasis. In answer to any other kind of question that would call for an opinion he would give a non-committal reply in as few words as possible, for fear of saying something with which I might not agree. If he were on his own when I called, conversation was more silence than words and Bill would never fill a silence. I used to try to sit him out, but it never worked; I always ended up having to say something.

Kathleen was another story. She was small, with a narrow face and hair cut short and straight across at the back. She was round-shouldered and winter or summer she wore a navy blue cardigan. When she spoke she did so with a half-sublimated quizzical smile, as if to take the harm out of it if she said the wrong thing. I could never quite work out if she was a hypochondriac or she had something wrong with her or both. She presented as obsequious, but underneath she was determined to conduct my visit her way. These visits were agony to me, but my sense of satisfaction at having done my duty was always immense.

I arrived at the cottage and knocked at the front door. The first time I called when new in the parish I had gone to the back door and Kathleen had directed me around to the front, where it took her the best part of five minutes to open the door swollen by the damp. Knowing she would do the same again I went to the front door, but I had no doubt that my visits were the only times it was ever opened. I had made a few attempts to suggest that I should use the back, as everyone else who came to the house did, but to no avail. This time there was no reply. I knew there was someone in and knocked again. I waited, and in due course Kathleen, after a brief struggle, opened the door. Bending forward she said:

'Rector,' and with determination in her eyes giving the lie to her quizzical smile she added, 'Come in.'

I stepped into the hall. She closed the door with as much difficulty as she had opened it and led the way into the sitting-room.

'I'd be happier to talk to you in the kitchen,' I said on principle, knowing I had some chance of relaxing sitting beside the cooker.

'I was just about to light the fire,' she said. It had probably not been lit since my last visit and I followed her into the tiny sitting-room with its low tongued and grooved ceiling and musty smell. The chintz-covered suite covered most of a strip of flowery brown and gold carpet and together with the table took up a fair portion of the room.

'No need to light the fire,' I said. 'It's warm.'

'I was about to light it anyway,' she lied again.

I had broken down every other family in the parish that had begun by treating me with this kind of formality, but Kathleen was as stubborn as she was neurotic.

I sat on the sofa and she went out to the kitchen to get matches. Damp began to penetrate the seat of my trousers. I looked around the room at the old sepia wedding photograph, hung within a few inches of the ceiling, a forgotten record of moments in the sun. Kathleen returned and put a firelighter under the paper and sticks in the grate. When the fire was established she put some coal on top, and rubbing her hands together sat back on an armchair. Without thinking I asked:

'How are you both keeping?' Making a lame attempt to produce a smile, she said:

'Bill is fine,' and with her face set to reinforce the bad news she was about to deliver, she launched into a litany of ills she had endured in the last year. From most of these she was still suffering, and she was determined to remain a martyr to them for the rest of her life. Suppressing a smile with difficulty, I said:

'Maybe things will improve with the fine weather and the long evenings.'

'The weather and the long evenings will have no effect,' she said frostily, 'when the doctors can't cure me.'

In an attempt to get off the subject of health and wellbeing I said:

'Did you know that the church will be a hundred and fifty years old this year, and we'll be having a celebration? Isn't it fascinating to think of all the people who worshipped there over the years?'

'Yes,' she said, 'and there aren't many of us left.'

At that moment the door opened and Bill came in from the kitchen. He touched his forelock and said:

'Hello, your reverence.'

'Hello, Bill,' I said. 'You're looking well. Kathleen tells me she hasn't had a good winter.' He jerked his head and raised his eyes heavenward, and said nothing.

'Wasn't it sad about Mr Leonard?' Kathleen said, claiming the initiative.

'It was indeed,' I said, 'and so young.'

'Shockin', shockin,' shockin,' and Bill added, 'The country's alive with it,' and he sat down on the other chair.

'I'm sorry we haven't been able to get to church lately,' Kathleen said, 'with not being well.'

'There's no need to apologise,' I said. 'Even if you were fit as a fiddle, you're free to make your own decisions. You have to decide these things for yourself.'

'For yourself, that's true,' said Bill.

'When you say your prayers,' I said to Kathleen, assuming without any reason to know that she did say prayers, and believing that she had less reason to have a difficulty in this department than I had, 'do you ask God to help with your problems?'

'Indeed I do, I have him tormented, asking him.'

'And does he help?' I asked.

'He does for a while, and then he seems to forget.'

By this time Bill had lit the pipe and had full steam up, adding to the smoke from the fire that was billowing back into the room from the cold chimney.

'Sorry about the smoke, it does that when the wind is in a certain quarter,' Kathleen said, as she got up and opened the window. She wasn't back in her chair before Bill got up and without a word slammed it shut. Neither said anything and there was another long silence that I broke with one of my repertoire of silence-breakers. Kathleen got up and left the room. Bill and I had one of our stop/go conversations until Kathleen eventually returned with a tea tray complete with cloth, wedding present delf and teapot to match. She poured a cup for me and then for Bill who looked distinctly uncomfortable managing the saucer. Kathleen offered me a plate of shop biscuits with:

'Sorry I have no cake, I didn't feel well enough to bake this week.'

The conversation staggered on until I became conscious again of the damp seat of my trousers and I decided to make a move. As I could have predicted, Kathleen said:

'You're not going yet, rector?'

'I'm afraid I must, I have another call to make before I get home,' I said lying in my teeth.

'I know you're busy,' she said leading the way to the hall door followed by Bill. 'How is your wife?' she asked with that cross between her quizzical smile and a smirk that accompanied almost everything she said and left me unsure, in the circumstances, of the true purpose of the question. Was she doing the socially correct thing by inquiring for Jennifer in a polite and general way, or was it prurience? Or was she really saying: 'We may be at the bottom of the pile in this parish but let me remind you we don't spend our time getting drunk in the pub.' It may have been a harmless enquiry for politeness sake, but given Kathleen's inscrutable personality, I couldn't be sure.

'Fine, thank you.' I said. 'It's good to see a stretch in the evenings,' which elicited from the two a rare expression of agreement. They stood at the door until I disappeared from sight. The visit had done the trick; I had done my duty and felt better for it and I wouldn't be back again for a year.

Chapter 7

S ince it was now clear that I could not avoid some kind of event to mark the anniversary of the church, I called a meeting of the select vestry.

The vestry was the usual mix of parishioners, but not representative of gender; there were twelve men and three women. Some were older members who knew exactly what the job was about, namely, to run the business affairs of the parish, and whose judgement was usually good. Some were those whose membership of the vestry was the only decision-making position they held, and, determined to make the most of it, nit-picked at every opportunity to the exasperation of the rest. Others were members of ability who were permanently puzzled by how it took so many people so long to make relatively trivial decisions. Then there were the ones who hadn't the confidence to say more than 'yes' or 'no' in public and didn't speak at all, but who had plenty to say outside after the meeting, where the real discussion of parish affairs took place.

The meeting was held in the rectory drawing room, which accommodated fifteen assorted chairs comfortably. Senior members sat in the same chairs meeting after meeting, and more recent members sat to the sides or at the back. One would not take off his coat, so that I fantasised that the backside was out of his trousers. Another always started by sitting on the arm of the sofa even though there were vacant seats. Another was incapable of sitting on a chair where it was: he had to move it six or eight inches one way or the other before he sat down.

Clergy can really only know parishioners insofar as they allow them to. A rector can be in a parish for many years and be unaware of the dark secrets of his parishioners unless they, or somebody else, choose to tell him. After a few years in a parish, however, a rector gets the hang of most of his parishioners; their style, their personalities and their own peculiar ways. Rectors value the helpful and co-operative ones, are content to work with the majority who support their parish, and curse under their breath the awkward, petty and stubborn ones and the ones who would wish them anywhere else but rector of their parish. There are usually a few parishioners with whom the rectory family is friendly and with whom they socialise outside the parish context and with some of these they become good friends. The select vestry in this case was representative of the parish, and there were among the membership people from each of these categories.

Earlier in the evening of the night of the meeting I lit the fire and gave the central heating a blast, on the principle that the more comfortable they were the more co-operative they would be. I did this with full knowledge of the risk I ran that if they were too comfortable they might dig in for a long session, for a vestry meeting was, for some of them, a night out. When we finally got through the other business I brought up the hundred and fiftieth anniversary of the church and Robert Armstrong's idea of a festival and his offer of two hundred and fifty pounds and redecoration.

'A hundred and fifty years,' somebody said, 'no wonder it needs a new roof.'

A few laughed and then the meeting fell silent. I was determined to keep my own counsel until I heard what they thought, and so the silence continued. Finally I asked them what we should do.

'Whatever we do,' another said, 'we should let him decorate the church and take the two hundred and fifty.' At this simple suggestion people smiled and there was general agreement.

'Mr Armstrong's offer is conditional on some kind of festival or celebration,' I reminded them.

'If he gives us the money won't we be celebrating anyway?' One of the smart Alec younger members said.

'If Mr Armstrong hadn't made his offer, would we be doing something?' one of the senior members asked.

'I was aware that the church was one hundred and fifty years old, but if he hadn't suggested it there wouldn't be a celebration,' I said.

'Now that he has brought it up, I suppose we'd better do something,' said the questioner.

'Why?' I asked provocatively.

'To get the two hundred and fifty and the church decorated.'

'There's no point decorating that church until the roof is done,' one said, 'could you go back and ask him if instead of decorating, he'd put on a new roof?' Everybody laughed.

'Let me be clear,' I said, 'the two hundred and fifty is for a celebration, whatever form it takes; it's not for the parish coffers.'

'Is it not our job to decide how parish money is spent?' asked the treasurer.

'It is of course,' I said, 'but it's not our money until we get it, and we won't get it unless we agree to spend it on a celebration.'

'Isn't he the right bollocks?' I overheard one of the younger ones whispering to his friend beside him and I assumed he was referring to Robert Armstrong and not to me.

'If we do have a celebration, what will we be celebrating?' asked one of the thoughtful ones. Another long silence.

'What do you think?' I asked, determined not to help.

'That Protestants are still alive and well and living in the countryside.'

'Do we need to have more reason than that the church is a hundred and fifty years old?' another asked. 'And whatever we do it should include the whole community.'

'I don't agree,' piped up the only bigot on the vestry. 'It's a Church of Ireland church.' It irritated me, but I let it pass, and I was glad nobody else took it up. I could see one particular member, who didn't often speak, winding himself up to say something, and when he had completed the rehearsal in his head of what he wanted to say, in the middle of somebody else speaking, he said:

'Couldn't we ask Mr Armstrong instead of painting the church to give the money towards a new roof?'

'We've already discussed that,' I said, impatiently and with a sharpness I regretted. He sat back in his chair deflated and sulked for the rest of the night, and no doubt vowed he'd never speak at a vestry meeting again. My concentration waned as there were two or three different discussions taking place at the same time, and I wasn't motivated to intervene. I withdrew inside my head and envisaged Jennifer in the kitchen, a small, bereft figure sitting beside the cooker, reading, waiting for me to tell her we were ready for tea. Jennifer insisted on providing tea and biscuits when there was a vestry meeting; she enjoyed talking to everybody while she served it; part of her sociable nature, rather than a sense of duty. I saw her as on a screen; at first I was in an emotional vacuum and felt neither love for her nor anger towards her. Then a deep sadness washed over me, which I tried to dispel by hoping she would somehow get help. My mind went back to my recent visit to Kate; the warmth of her welcome and the ease with which we talked and the comfortable feeling I had just being with her.

I could hear in the distance the animated conversation in the room. I didn't want to rejoin the meeting and allowed my mind to wander. I didn't really care what they decided to do about the church. It didn't bother me if it was never painted or if the roof fell in. The building held no place in my scheme of faith; it didn't contribute one whit to what I believed, neither did it take from it. I did appreciate it as a good example of a stone church of its period, but I couldn't help feeling that sooner or later it would end up being deconsecrated and used as a residence or a restaurant or that it would become a dignified ruin.

It belonged to the parishioners, the majority of whom had been born and brought up in the parish, and were baptised, and for some, married in it, and whose parents and grandparents were buried in the churchyard. For them its connection with the historic Christian faith was tenuous, but its emotional significance as their tribal shrine was enormous. There was no point in asking them to think, or asking them to learn more about the Christian faith. That was for me to do. Change nothing, was the principle that governed their religious lives, do things as they had always been done, for the Church, as Fred Leonard would have said, ought to be the one unchanging place of refuge from the complexities and tensions of the ever-changing modern world. I wished I could have been like them. Well, I didn't really, but it would have saved me a great deal of trouble.

Was there a middle way? There was no doubt in my mind they were, largely speaking, good people. There were of course in the parish all the social and family problems that there are anywhere, and I saw the inside of many of them. None the less they were, by and large, God-fearing family people who cared for their children, worked hard and paid their bills. Until Jennifer began spending so much money on drink, I too paid my debts, was God-fearing in my own terms and for me my family had priority over everything else, and yet, in what I believed, I was poles apart from them. If I had not been ordained and had stayed in the bank I would be living a comfortable middle-class life in a city suburb, working nine to five and a maybe a little bit more, five days a week, and the rest of my time would be my own. I would be responsible to myself for what I thought and believed, and I would not have to endure Mrs Bowers and her flower jars or Robert Armstrong and his scheme to affirm himself and his family. I could understand his sadness that there wasn't anyone to inherit, but I had no time for him bribing the parish and me to make a fuss to mark the anniversary of his family church. On the other hand, if I weren't in the ministry, neither would I have all the fulfilment of being with people in their joys and the satisfaction of supporting them in their sorrows, in this wonderful, often cruel, but above all, mysterious life. Mrs Bowers and Robert Armstrong, and all the other torments of parish life were a small price to pay for that.

I rejoined the meeting as the man in the parish who had the inside story on everything was pumping his arm up and down like the handle of a yard pump, to drive home the truth of what he was saying:

'…she definitely made a mistake, but they can't ask for the medals back now.' I waited to pick up the thread.

'She won't be asked again,' another said. They were discussing a mistake one of the judges made at the community games that caused civil war in the village. I waited for an opportunity and said:

'Can we get back to the matter of the church?' and noticed two people simultaneously looking at their watches. They were no further on.

'We'll have to have the bishop for a big service,' somebody said. It was the first time I heard mention of other than money, painting and the church roof. The rambling was just about to get going again, when I suggested what I had planned anyway; that they appoint a sub-committee to run the anniversary celebrations. They all agreed, which meant that most of them would have someone else to blame when there was criticism from parishioners or if things went wrong. Most of them were glad to have their say, but doing anything about it was another matter. Four members agreed to serve on the sub-committee and I agreed to chair it. We closed the meeting with the customary touching of the forelock to the Almighty, by saying the Grace, and I left them to get on with the news, gossip and scandal of the parish and district as I went to the kitchen to tell Jennifer we were ready for tea.

Jennifer was asleep beside the cooker. I didn't want to disturb her, so I raised the cooker lid and lifted the kettle across onto the hot ring. I took one of the trays of cups and biscuits from the table and was as far as the door when Jennifer woke.

'I'll do that,' she said and came over, took the tray from me and went into the drawing room. One of the women came back to the kitchen with her to collect the other tray while Jennifer waited for the kettle to boil. I went back into the drawing room and sat beside two women who had been elected to the sub-committee.

The women of farming families are often more interesting than the men. Many of them come from farms themselves, stay on at school and then leave home and qualify at something; nursing, teaching or as secretaries. They then marry men, many of whom knowing they were coming home to the farm didn't make much effort at school and left as soon as possible, and could talk knowledgeably about nothing but farming, machinery and cars.

Ann and Valerie had both been away, qualified as teacher and nurse and both had married back into farms where their husbands had been since leaving school early. They were good friends and went to events in the parish together. I got on well with both of them, because they were affable, honest and good fun.

'You're not keen on this festival,' Ann challenged me.

'Was it that obvious?'

'I'm afraid it was,' said Valerie.

'Well it's true,' I said, 'I'm not sure what it is we have to celebrate.'

'Does it matter?' asked Valerie, 'It's an excuse for something different. A break in routine is good for everybody.'

'You've been talking to Jennifer,' I said, 'but if we're saying the celebration is a thanksgiving for a hundred and fifty years of Christian witness, I'm not so sure.'

'What do you mean?' Ann asked.

'The people who built that church were part of the political system that enforced the penal laws that proscribed the Roman Catholic religion. They enforced a whole series of laws designed to make Catholics second-class citizens and to keep them down in their own country.'

'That's all in the past and best forgotten,' said Valerie, 'those days are long gone.'

'I know they are, but if we are celebrating a hundred and fifty years of the church, in addition to thanking God for all that was good in the Church's life, we ought also to ask God for forgiveness for all that was bad.'

'That's fair enough,' said Valerie, 'that's all right by me, but it need not stop us doing something.'

'What I don't want,' I said, 'is anything that smacks of exclusiveness. If we celebrate we celebrate as part of the whole community. Our past is part of us, this is the way we are, the bad as well as the good, but none of us can be held responsible for the wrongs our ancestors did, nor can we take credit for the good they did either.'

'You take it all so seriously,' said Ann, 'I don't think people will see it like that.'

'I don't know if they will or not. It's as hard for a community to see itself as others see it as it is for an individual. There is a lot of goodwill, as you know, amongst Catholics in the countryside for the

Protestant community and vice versa and we must be careful to avoid anything thoughtless that might injure that.'

Our conversation was interrupted by a shemozzle at the other end of the room. Ted Saunders was a prosperous bachelor farmer in his early sixties, who over the years had put together a fine acreage of land. He was a puritan Protestant, a measured, cautious and careful man who looked at both sides of every penny before he spent it. He didn't smoke or drink and considered Sunday newspapers the work of the devil. In fact he wouldn't take the car out on a Sunday except to go to church and always arranged for his workman to come in on Sundays to feed the cattle. He had absolutely no doubt in his mind that his material prosperity was a reward from God for what he saw as his exemplary life.

Ted was standing up hopping from one foot to the other and holding his trousers out from himself as well as he could. Jennifer had knocked a cup of scalding tea right into his lap and he looked for all the world as though he had wet himself. People, inhibited in the circumstances from helping, were offering him handkerchiefs, which he declined, intent upon holding the wet area away from himself. Eventually he put his own handkerchief down inside the front of his trousers and his slightly calmer demeanour showed that he had achieved some relief. The whole performance was accompanied by protestations of apology from Jennifer, which Ted ignored either because he was preoccupied with keeping the scalding tea away from his vulnerable area or because he chose not to accept them.

Jennifer went out to the kitchen to get a towel and I brought Ted out after her. He wiped himself with the towel and decided the best thing was to get home as quickly as possible.

'I'll go,' he said.

Jennifer apologised again, 'I really don't know how it happened.'

'Good night,' he blustered, and without acknowledging the apology he made for the door. I saw him to his car and said how sorry I was.

'She couldn't hold the cup of tea with the shake in her hand,' he said, and drove off. I was taken aback by his impertinence.

'You self-righteous bastard,' I said out loud, as I watched the lights disappear around the bend of the avenue. I stood for a minute in the bright frosty night and admired the stars in the cloudless sky, trying to get my mind around the immensity of the universe and, aware of my own insignificance, I went back inside.

The others were beginning to drift away, and Ann and Valerie were chatting with Jennifer. I went into the drawing room, checked the fire and tidied the chairs. When everyone had gone Jennifer and I sat down in the kitchen. This was just the kind of time, in normal circumstances, that I would have liked a stiff drink.

'You chose the wrong one to scald,' I said.

'Or maybe the right one, depending which way you look at it,' Jennifer said with a laugh.

'Of all people,' I said, and thought of telling her what he had said as he drove away, but decided against it.

'What are they doing about a festival for the church?' Jennifer asked.

'They've appointed a sub-committee to plan and run it.'

'Who are they?'

'Ann and Valerie, John Brink and Willie Moreland.'

'Ann and Valerie will be good, but the other two won't have much to contribute.'

At a time when we were having a conversation like this I felt pity for Jennifer, as I knew it was only an interlude in a life governed by an obsession with alcohol. I knew that she would not allow me closer than this polite kind of conversation, lest I try to come between her and the means of satisfying her addiction. I hoped for a future for us and saw myself as staying in touch so that I could help when the time came. Though feeling a great emotional distance between us now, I had an image in my mind of falling in love with Jennifer again, as I imagined people did after an affair had ended. As far as I was concerned she was having an affair with alcohol.

Despite the numbness, the hope that she would recover kept me going, and in the meantime the parish kept me busy. How much I would want the parish when she became sober I did not know, but when the time came I would re-evaluate everything. When I thought like this it excited me, and I hoped each bad night might be her last. Every night of Jennifer's drinking was eroding our future together that, whatever way I looked at it, would be a much shorter time than the past we had shared. I found myself frequently quantifying time in this way using normal life expectancy, which I could reasonably estimate, but unable to estimate how long Jennifer would go on drinking. I could not guess at it, but hoped it would not be much longer.

The centenary celebrations of the church seemed to have caught Jennifer's imagination. It was like her student enthusiasms, but of less intensity. She wouldn't have seen the celebrations as Robert Armstrong saw them, nor indeed as most of the parishioners would, but as a sign of life in the dozy parish, and that some show of enthusiasm would indicate that the parishioners were real live people after all.

'Did they make any suggestions?' she asked.

'Don't you know? They suggested everything in the way of anything that was ever done in a parish before; a fête, a sports day, a flower festival, a barbecue and any other social event that is stock-in-trade of your average country parish. They even asked me if I'd write a history of the parish.'

'That's a good idea. Why don't you? It would be an interest.'

' "The cobbler to his last." I'm not a historian, and I certainly don't feel competent to write a history of the parish, especially since so much of the early years would be a history of the Armstrong family.'

Jennifer and I hadn't had a conversation like this for a long time, even in Lent when she wasn't drinking. I felt a normality I hadn't felt for ages. We were communicating without edge and without evasion, and so I plucked up courage and broached the problem.

'Jennifer, can we talk about us?'

'What do you mean?'

'We've lost touch with each other. This is the first normal conversation we've had for ages.'

'That's because I have to drag every word out of you. You're not the slightest bit interested in this anniversary event. You think it's beneath you.'

'That's not true, but I don't want to go into that now. I want to talk about us.'

'Well, what do you want to say?'

'That we've grown apart. We used to spend more time together, especially since the children went. Other than meals we're leading independent lives.'

'That's because you're out so much. You've never worked so hard in the parish.'

'That's because you're seldom here and when you are you're either sleeping or recovering.'

'What do you mean?'

'You know very well what I mean.'

'If you're referring to the fact that I go out for a few drinks, I've told you before; it's because you're never here and I have to have some company.' Jennifer had developed this technique so that when the subject of her drinking looked like coming up she projected the problem onto me. Here it was again; it was all my fault.

'You know in your heart and soul that that's not true. The reason you go out so much is to drink, and to try to blame me simply isn't fair.'

'Are you saying that I'm devious? Well maybe it's you that's the devious one excusing the fact that you're never at home because I'm out.' It was true that I was out of the house more recently than I used to be because either Jennifer wasn't there, or if she was she was no company and best left alone. She had done it again; she had turned it back on me.

I couldn't look Jennifer straight in the eye these days, simply because she wouldn't let me. On this occasion, insofar as I could, with my tone of voice I did look her straight in the eye and said:

'Jennifer your drinking is out of hand, and only you can do something about it.'

'If you don't get off this subject I'm going,' she spat back. I got up and stood with my back to the door and with anger in my voice that surprised her and even surprised me, I said:

'You haven't the guts to face up to the truth. You have a serious drink problem and you need help, but nobody can help unless you ask for it.'

'Are you saying that I'm an alcoholic?' I was determined that this was going to be a full frontal attack. This time I was not going to pull punches.

'That's precisely what I'm saying, and you haven't got the moral courage to face up to it.' She pushed her chair back, stood up and came over to me. With steely eyes and incandescent with rage, she leaned forward to within a few inches and shouted into my face:

'I'm not a fucking alcoholic, and if I were I wouldn't want to be diagnosed by an amateur psychologist like you that knows bugger all about it,' and she turned and stormed out the other door into the garden.

I had never seen Jennifer so angry. Normally when she was cross she could express it with words alone; a few well-chosen words, spoken in a measured tone, that went straight to the heart of the matter and left nobody in any doubt where she stood. Until recently no topic had been off-limits for discussion; with her sharp mind she would evaluate issues and give a carefully considered response. In recent times, however, by every signal she sent out she had proscribed any mention of her drinking. My violation of this prohibition had unleashed an anger that could have come from nothing other than a perceived threat to her survival.

I did not see it that way but I was on the outside looking in, which gave me a very different perspective from hers. I couldn't imagine what I hadn't experienced, I had never had to struggle with an addiction, but I was shattered by her anger. I found that my legs were weak. I held the rail of the cooker with both hands and tried to convince myself that my attempt to talk to her about her problem had been justified. I sat down, put my head in my hands and felt a great emptiness.

Chapter 8

Frosty spring evenings became warm summer nights. Parish activities wound slowly down for the summer season, leaving me more time for reflection.

Altogether apart from Jennifer's problem, on and off during the previous few years my struggle with what I believed, or to be more precise, what I didn't believe, became more acute. I had always been a doubting Thomas, but I had recently found myself more and more unable to subscribe to much of orthodox Christian doctrine. I had great difficulty saying the Creed in church and comforted myself by saying that it was simply a statement of faith of the fourth century Christian community, with which the Church is in continuity. I felt no obligation to express my own beliefs in the terms of the Creed, but was prepared to subscribe to it as an historic document. As I continued to explore what I believed I began to question whether I really did want to identify with the fourth century Church of Nicea, a Council called and manipulated by the Emperor. I had no difficulty about Jesus and his teaching, other than how to understand him as God, or even Son of God, but I had great difficulty with many of the princes, prelates and preachers of the Church ever since, and what they taught.

I had been finding it harder and harder to meet the expectation that parishioners, both consciously and unconsciously, laid upon me. Their expectation was that I should reinforce them in their own prejudices and understanding of the faith. This it seemed to me was a simplistic belief that God was a white Anglo-Saxon Protestant with a particular affection for the Church of Ireland who looked down benevolently when they were being honest and behaving well and was displeased, but would forgive them when they were behaving badly. In trouble, if they prayed earnestly enough, he would get them out of their problem by intervening, especially in matters of health. Most of them believed that if they prayed, God would intervene in the weather, not quite that he would give them rain in one field and sun in the one beside it, but that he would send rain or fine weather to meet their farming needs. It didn't seem to be a problem that he didn't intervene to save the lives of millions of people throughout the world who were dying as a result of drought, especially little children dying through no fault of their own. How they accounted for this kind of favouritism on God's part I do not know.

I could not bring myself to reinforce people in this kind of religion if this was what they did believe. I could only glean what they believed from things they said in passing. I had no way of being sure, since most of them were reluctant to respond to opportunities, formal or informal, to talk about it. I suspected that many of them thought that, unlike themselves, I knew it all and believed it all, and that it was my job to know and believe on their behalf. As long as I was there to do it for them they would leave it to me, thereby making it unnecessary to think for themselves. If I were to leave they would simply provide the free house and regulation stipend for another rector to do the same.

These, despite their simple faith, or maybe because of it, were good people. I had no doubt that most of them were, by nature, superior Christians to me in their natural kindness, generosity and neighbourliness, and in their largely uncomplicated lives. What right had I to upset them with my own theological confusion?

My doubts and uncertainties were real. They didn't bother me other than that I had to conduct the liturgy which assumed beliefs I didn't have. Apart from the creed many of the hymns we sang every Sunday were incredible. The tunes were good and they had positive emotional associations with childhood, but the words were appalling. I did read modern theology and was able to convert some theological thought forms of other eras into modern theological concepts. Slowly, however, I was coming to the conclusion that this process could only go so far and that what I actually believed and did not believe put me outside the orthodox teaching of the Church and a hundred miles away from most parishioners. No matter what way I looked at it, I didn't believe in a God that intervened in the natural order. I certainly couldn't believe in, for example, the virgin birth or the bodily resurrection as historical events, and I had no doubt in my own mind that there was no life after death.

I knew the modern theological answers to these kinds of problems, but these answers did not convince me that they were in conformity with the teaching of the early Church or of Church doctrine. I found theological debate, with modern theological insights, stimulating on the rare occasions when I could get one of my colleagues to discuss them with me. I found, however, that most of my colleagues weren't the slightest bit interested in discussing these things, and some of them made it plain that they didn't know what my difficulty was. Some of them had the 'what's-the-problem?' attitude to the extent that they made me feel foolish so that I had long since stopped trying to get their opinion on anything. Others patronised me by telling me that modern theology had moved on a long way from where I was and the issues I presented, and that my difficulties were old hat. My response to this was that if I did express my ideas in obsolete theological terms, the thing to do was to point out the progression from where I was to where things had come to today. Some of them, as they patronised me, stopped just short of ridicule. One did actually tell me that I really ought not to air such views, as theologically informed people would laugh at me. All of this caused me to retreat into my shell and struggle with these things on my own. I used to be able to discuss them with Jennifer, but these days she was struggling with her own demon and had lost patience with mine.

Now that summer was here I had no excuse; I had all the time in the world to sort myself out before embarking on preparations for the church anniversary celebrations in October. The one thing I did have to do before my holidays was to convene the vestry sub-committee to begin to make plans.

The sub-committee met in the rectory after the first cut of silage. Ensconced in the study the four looked to me to come up with ideas, but I was determined not to take the initiative. I would support them and help them to sort out the best thing to do, but I would not do it for them. Jennifer was right, Ann and Valerie would have good ideas and would do the work, while John and Willie would not be much help.

John, in his early thirties, was country cute, so that though I wouldn't have given much for my chances of bettering him in a deal, I knew that he wasn't bright enough to make a constructive contribution, and he wasn't aware enough to conceal the fact. While on the other hand Willie was one of those farmers who by intelligence and hard work had built up a fine farm of land. He was almost entirely uneducated, but suffered under the illusion that his success in farming qualified him to pontificate on almost every subject under the sun apart from brain surgery, and even on that he wouldn't be backward about venturing an opinion.

After a long silence Ann kicked off:

'Are we sure we want to have celebrations at all?' hoping finally to lay to rest my reservations. The two men said nothing.

'The vestry gave us the go-ahead,' said Valerie. 'Isn't that why we're here?'

Another silence. I ended this one by asking John what he thought.

'I think we should do something,' he said.

'What do you think?' I asked Willie, who launched into a convoluted anecdote from his early years in farming. It was designed to illustrate some point to do with the proposed festival and it was no harm if in passing it showed how well he had done in life. So as not to ignore altogether what he said, I asked:

'Given what you say, what are we going to do?' And before he could answer I fibbed:

'I have a phone call to make. Jot down your ideas and I'll be back in a minute.'

I handed a note pad and pencil to Ann and went out to the kitchen and left them to it. They had plenty to work with from the suggestions made at the vestry meeting, so I didn't feel I was landing them in it completely. I was fed up leading from the front, and as long as I would do it, parishioners would let me. On this occasion I was determined they should take the initiative, and I would give them all the support I could. I sat for about twenty minutes in the kitchen before going back to the study.

The other three were talking and as I sat down Ann whispered to me with a grin:

'That was a long phone call!' knowing well my ploy, and then added at normal volume: 'We're not much further on,' feeling some responsibility, since she had the pencil and paper. 'We are agreed on one thing; that there should be a service with the bishop present and preaching. It should be ecumenical with Fr Keane and Fr Kelly invited to take part and neighbouring rectors invited. We'd like it to be open to all, and have it announced in the Catholic church too, but if we did that everybody wouldn't fit.' Valerie added: 'We could have the annual parish dinner dance around the same time, and as many as wanted could come to that.'

'That's a good idea,' said John.

'There you have it; one religious and one social event,' said Willie, feeling, no doubt, that all this was beneath a man of his experience, and hoping the meeting would be soon over.

'I'm sure the teachers would do something with the children in the school, maybe a concert, or even posters,' Ann offered.

'What about the suggestion at the vestry meeting that the rector write a parish history?' asked John.

'No bloody fear.' I thought to myself. 'My take on the history of the parish wouldn't go down well.' 'I'm afraid not,' I said, 'I'm not a historian; there's more to writing a parish history than you think, if it's to be well done. If you really want to do that you could commission someone to do it, but it would take time and cost money.'

'Haven't we got the two hundred and fifty pounds Mr Armstrong is giving?' said John, without thinking, and Willie soon put him straight on that one.

'We'll need all that and more,' but he didn't say what for. Spending money on a parish history would be throwing money down the drain as far as Willie was concerned. He saw the financial implications of everything, and added:

'It's making money for the parish the celebrations should be, not costing us.'

Nobody challenged him. Everybody knew him too well. Willie paid more attention to the parish finances than the treasurer, and seemed to think that the sole criterion for judging the success of a parish was money in the bank.

'Where are we now?' asked Ann, 'we have a service, a dance and the children in the school to do something. Is there anything else?' No response. 'If there are any more bright ideas we can meet again.' They picked two successive Friday nights in October for the service and the dance. They didn't want the service on a Sunday to ensure the bishop and the other clergy could come, and there would be some kind of supper in the hall afterwards.

As soon as we had finished Willie and John left and Ann and Valerie sat on to chat. I was fond of them both; they treated me like an ordinary human being rather than a clergyman. I was glad of their company. They were both aware of Jennifer's problem, and without saying a word I knew they understood and were not at all judgemental. They were two of a small number of parishioners Jennifer and I had become friends with. After a while we adjourned to the kitchen and made coffee.

Returning to her question to me after the vestry meeting Ann said: 'You still haven't told me why you are not enthusiastic about the celebrations.'

'I don't really know. I'm not even keen on birthdays and anniversaries,' wanting to show that my lack of enthusiasm wasn't to do only with the parish. 'People should celebrate when they feel like it, when they are in the mood, and not because a certain date comes around on the calendar. The importance of the past is that it can help us to understand the present, and no matter who we are we all have bad bits as well as good in our past, whether as individuals or as communities. I am happy that there are lots of good things in the history of this parish, but the building of that church wasn't one of them. It was a bit of triumphalism at the expense of people whose own religion was proscribed, and who had to meet for their own worship in glens and behind hills around the countryside. The trouble was that in those days whoever was in power tolerated only their own way of believing and everyone else's way was outlawed. If I was right you must be wrong; the blasphemy of certainty. The essence of Protestantism is freedom of conscience, but in those days that freedom didn't include other people's right to disagree. Thank God we've all moved on since then. The real division these days is between people who work things out for themselves and those who want to be told by somebody else what to believe.'

'What in the name of goodness has all that to do with the anniversary of the church?' Ann asked.

'Nothing if you just want an excuse for a party, and maybe you're right, that's what it should be: a party without asking the 'whys' and 'wherefores.''

Keep life simple. If the parish wanted a party, that was all right with me. I was just amused when I thought of the different reasons for the celebration: Robert Armstrong, to affirm himself and his family; Willie, to make money for the parish; Ann to have a bit of a party, and no doubt there were many more. I should have seen the purpose as praising God for his goodness to the parish and celebrating all the parishioners, good ones, not so good ones and the shysters that worshipped there over the years, but that kind of thing wasn't in my theological repertoire.

Once again I had to remind myself not to project my own approach onto the parish, but to facilitate them to be themselves and move on. I had no right to impose my way of thinking onto others, although I suspected there was a small number of parishioners who thought like me. I believed, however, that if people had a strong faith they could handle questions I might ask, or else ignore them. To show willing I said:

'I'll write to the bishop and contact the other clergy, if you'll look after the dance.' They agreed and I said I would also talk to the teachers about the children doing something. I didn't want Ann and Valerie to leave; I was enjoying their company. There was a break in the conversation when we had made the arrangements and I offered them more coffee. Neither wanted more.

'We'd better go,' Valerie said, 'it's late.'

At that moment I heard a noise in the yard. As they stood up to leave Jennifer came in the back door. She was earlier than her usual time and as far as I could see she was sober.

'Hello Ann, hello Valerie, have you had a good meeting? What delights have you arranged for the festival?'

'A service, a dance and the school to do something,' I said.

'No doubt his Lordship will be present?' Jennifer enquired. I could see it coming. I thought she was about to launch into one of her diatribes against the bishop, but instead she took up the sweeping brush and turning it head up she paraded with solemn affectation down the kitchen forcing smiles and nodding pompously left and right. She put down the brush and without a word she went over to the cooker and put on the kettle.

'Anyone for coffee?' she asked, taking a biscuit from the table. 'My God, that man. I don't know how he has the neck to come down here and parade like a peacock, when he doesn't know the first thing about what's going on in the parish. He doesn't seem to care since he never asks, and when he is here for an event he spends his time telling us how busy he is. His clergy and their wives could be starving to death or having affairs all over the countryside and he wouldn't know the first thing about it.'

'He's not a bad sort really,' I said, conscious of Ann and Valerie who wouldn't be familiar with the clergy and rectory family perspective on the bishop. 'The Church uses her bishops badly,' I added, 'expecting them to turn up to every bun fight and the blessing of every parish pump in the diocese.'

'That doesn't excuse them from their pastoral responsibility for the clergy and their families,' Jennifer said, 'our one has about as much pastoral sense as a sharp stick.'

Jennifer was right. The bishop came into the parish for an occasion and never asked how we were or what we were up to. I did think, however, that subconsciously she was projecting responsibility for her own problem away from herself and onto him. If, however, he had shown an interest she would undoubtedly have told him in no uncertain terms it was none of his business. If he ever did decide to play the game, it is certain he could never win.

'Should we ask him at all if he's that busy?' asked Ann. 'Does an anniversary service come under the heading of blessing a parish pump?'

'Of course we should ask him; it's one of his churches. If he can't come let him make his own excuses,' Jennifer came back.

'I'm sure he'll come if he can,' I said, trying to take the harm out of what Jennifer had said.

Valerie and Ann got up to leave. Jennifer and I went with them and stood on the step outside. It was a clear summer night. We stood for a while after they had gone, picking out and naming stars.

I put my arm around Jennifer's shoulder, which was no more than skin and bone.

'You were early tonight.'

'I was with Kate. She wanted to talk. Conor has been in touch, he wants a divorce.'

'How does Kate feel about that?'

'I think she's half relieved. The longer it went on the more she thought this was likely, and she's glad the uncertainty is over. She can now get on with the rest of her life. For the first year or so she thought there was hope, but she has since discounted the possibility of a reconciliation. I think she's sad more for Siobhán than for herself.'

I knew something of what Kate must have felt. Jennifer and I, although living together, were estranged. Jennifer had left me for alcohol some years before, and although I still felt there was hope she might come back, that hope was diminishing with every day that passed. 'Hope springs eternal in the human breast,' and in my better moments I held on desperately to it.

Looking up to the night sky Jennifer said. 'I wonder does God ever regret making humans; we're making such a mess of things.'

'Or if you want to look at it that way,' I said, 'he could have forgiven Adam and Eve and left them in the garden.'

Chapter 9

When the children were small we spent holidays in a caravan or cottage at the sea in exchange for Sunday and emergency duty, and hoped nobody would die during the time we were there. It was an economical holiday and Mary and Peter loved the seaside. Jennifer was great with them; she could play as one of them and enter into their world. She invented games and things to do that absorbed all three of them for hours on end. I joined in when they needed a fourth, but more often watched, or sat and read. In those days I used to look forward to when Mary and Peter's education was finished and we could afford holidays that were not self-catering and would allow me Sundays off, since I found taking services the most stressful part of the job. By the time the children were self-sufficient, that now all pervading factor in our lives, Jennifer's drinking, meant we still couldn't afford a proper holiday.

That year we went to mind the house for Mary and her husband Tom in the city, while they went on holiday to the sun. At least there was no Sunday duty and it was an opportunity to see some of our old college friends. We were packed and ready to go when Jennifer declaimed:

'I don't know why we're going up here; it's just exchanging one sink for another.'

'We've been over this before,' I said crossly, 'it's the best we can afford because you spend so much of our money on alcohol.' I had become more direct and adopted a policy of missing no opportunity to confront her when it seemed appropriate. Now I always used the word 'alcohol' rather than 'drink,' in the hope that the word would seep through to her brain. In retrospect a naive hope that anything so painless might confront the addiction that was consuming her life.

I wasn't depressed. I didn't suffer from that blackness that over the years I had heard depressed people describe, but everything was a uniform grey; there was no colour and no brightness. There were no highs or lows in my life, no mountains or valleys, just a barren waste stretching ahead into a grey haze on the horizon. My life was in suspense waiting and hoping, and sometimes losing hope to the point that I despaired of ever being in touch with Jennifer again. I tried to protect her from the gossip of parishioners and people in the village, but it was difficult and indeed impossible when she was away from me. I dreaded to think how she behaved in the village at night, but that was outside my control. I supported her when I was able and I could do no more. We lived separate lives apart from sharing meals that for some reason Jennifer was meticulous about. Perhaps it was her way of claiming normality or more likely the way she justified having the money she spent in the pub.

I was apprehensive about two weeks together in a small suburban house with so much free time. On the other hand I had to get away from the rectory and the phone. It was impossible between callers and the phone to be on holiday in the rectory, and I wasn't prepared to leave Jennifer on her own. She did not respond to my blaming her and her drinking for the exchange of one sink for another, but she said:

'You'll be bored stiff after a week and want to come home,' which was a possibility, as I sometimes found holidays without a particular purpose boring. It would, however, take me about a week to wind down and I would only begin to benefit on the second week. The most pleasurable part of some holidays was coming home. Anyway we had made the arrangement with Mary and we had to honour our commitment.

We packed the car and left around mid-day. As Jennifer always walked to and from the village we were seldom in the car together, and apart from mealtimes, which were often interrupted by the telephone, we seldom had time to talk at length. From some throw-away comments she made on the journey I sensed that Jennifer felt trapped. I tried to imagine how she felt exchanging her familiar haunts and her drinking companions for the uncertainty of different territory and having me around all day. Her opportunities to drink would be limited. I wondered was she planning strategies to get away on her own or would she do what she did in Lent and stay off it for the two weeks.

At home or with friends she never drank too much. In fact the very opposite; she would nurse one drink for a whole evening while everyone else had two or three, as if to confound anyone who thought she had a problem. Jennifer knew I liked a couple of drinks, but I didn't like pubs. I had my fill of talking to people in my work in the parish so when I relaxed I liked to be on my own or with particular friends. She did like the pub atmosphere and was quite happy to talk to strangers. She had the kind of outgoing personality that people responded to readily; she took people as she found them and was more tolerant of 'pub talk' than I was. The one thing she could not abide was pretence of any kind, and would expose it without mercy. She was completely intolerant of anyone who put on an accent. She was hilarious when imitating clergy who had a special voice for conducting the liturgy, as though God didn't approve of regional accents.

'What do you plan to do while we're in Dublin?' she asked after a long silence.

'The only plan I have is to get away from the phone and the door bell.'

'That's not very positive. It only says what you want to escape from, not what you want to do.'

'I want to wander down to the shop for the paper, and to take time over breakfast reading it, to know that nobody will knock at the door looking for something or other, to know that when the telephone rings it's not for me. To know that my time is my own and to feel that I can be entirely myself, that's a holiday for me.'

'How unimaginative, how dull.'

'Well what do you want to do?'

'I want to see a film or two, go to the theatre, wander round the Gallery, go to the Concert Hall, and maybe have a meal with Derek and Heather if they're not away. I want to do things we can't do at home. That's what a holiday is for.'

Jennifer did make my expectation of the holiday sound dull compared with hers, but then she didn't have to put up with the constant demands of parishioners, day after day. She didn't have to smooth ruffled feathers or be careful to choose the discreet or diplomatic word and to fight the unspoken battle I fought to keep the parish from being parochial and parishioners from regressing into the false sense of security of the folk religion of a minority tribe. I needed time to reclaim myself, my real self, the self buried beneath the heap of rubbish that parishioners dump upon the clergy, before I'd have energy for concerts, films or theatre.

Mary and Tom had left the house spick and span, and a list of instructions on how to work the television and the washing machine, and a note to say that if we weren't too busy maybe we'd have time to cut the grass. The first night we indulged the novelty of numerous television channels and went to bed early. Next morning Jennifer phoned Derek and Heather, who were Jennifer's closest friends at university.

Derek was an engineer and now a successful businessman. Heather had done maths in the same year as Jennifer and had gone on to be an actuary. After their children were grown she went back to work. We saw them occasionally and although Derek and I hadn't much in common, he was pleasant, and we got on well together. On the rare occasions that Jennifer was in town she met Heather for lunch. The arrangement they made was that they would pick us up on Friday to go out for a meal.

Our days took on a routine; up late, out for lunch, into town, down the pier or up the hills for a walk. In the evenings Jennifer went to a film or theatre, and to my surprise came straight home. In the second week I would go with her, but for the moment I was content to fall asleep in front of the television. We became relaxed with each other in a way we hadn't been for some time. When we went to a pub for lunch Jennifer never had more than one drink; she was in her I'll-show-you-I-haven't-a-problem mode. The more I saw of the old Jennifer the more I began to hope. I fantasised about a normal future for us, and dared to think that Jennifer might get a glimpse of it too. We were both looking forward to our night out with Derek and Heather.

On Friday morning after breakfast Jennifer went on her long-planned visit to the Gallery. It was something I could take in small doses, but I couldn't spend most of the day there as Jennifer would. In the afternoon it was sunny and warm and I took a bus out of town to a beach an hour from the city, and walked along the water's edge. Living in the heart of the country I missed the sea; its immensity, the sound of its ceaseless wave action and its tides that put us in touch with the moon and the planets and the infinities of the universe. The sea, as always, heightened my awareness of these mysteries, and gave me a sense of the numinous that Church worship seldom did. The same sea could be unspeakably cruel, when, driven by its equally cruel and unpredictable partner, wind, it marauds in mountainous billows and draws down into its unfathomable depths voyagers who dare to take it for granted. At other times under clear blue sky, in the absence of its partner in crime, it can be still and glistening like a vast sheet of glass, presenting a face of tranquillity, a deceptive face of innocence.

As I walked along the shore the sea was neither of these, but somewhere in between. A strong breeze blew up and drove an endless supply of clouds across the sky. It whipped up a moderate swell that broke on the beach leaving foam to disperse slowly on the sand until it was covered by the succeeding wave of the incoming tide. The sun came through intermittently but not enough to counter the chill sea breeze; I was glad I had worn a jacket. I tried to see the sea as primitive man might have seen it, without the scientific knowledge we take for granted. I had heard of children brought up in the country seeing the sea for the first time and being fearful of it. At times like this I felt attuned to the mystery of creation, for which I had awesome reverence and respect. Whatever caused the whole thing, we had a responsibility to look after it and each other as part of it and this was a full-time job for anybody. Obsession with personal salvation is the ultimate selfishness. When saving one's own soul is the priority, it divides off people from others who have a different understanding of salvation, or none at all. The pursuit of personal salvation drives wedges between people and makes everything else secondary to the extent of alienating friend from friend and even to dividing families.

The greyness of my recent humour had lifted a little and I was feeling more in tune with something. With what, I wasn't sure. I turned around at the far end of the beach and walked back. I looked wistfully at the immensity of the sea and knew it could relieve me of all my anxiety and waiting. I had heard of people who had committed suicide by simply walking into the water and I could understand that, without having the inclination to do it myself. I did think, however, if ever I were inclined, that it was the way to go. I sat at the foot of one of the dunes at the top of the beach and contemplated nothing more than the random thoughts that entered my mind. I was more at peace with the world and myself than I had been for a long while; I was in sympathy with everybody and everything. At just after five o'clock I walked to the road and waited for a bus. I resented the intrusion of the busy world into my contemplation. Travelling in the opposite direction to the rush hour traffic coming bumper-to-bumper from town, I was back in earnest in the real world. Stopped at a red light I looked at my watch and in the midst of hordes of business people on their way home from work I thought of my farmer parishioners some of whom would now be just about to start the evening milking.

I was back before Jennifer. We had about two hours before Derek and Heather were due to pick us up. I put mugs and a milk jug on a tray, made a pot of tea and took them to the sitting room to watch the news. I woke twenty minutes later having missed the news and my untouched mug of tea was cold. I went to the kitchen, poured it out, added hot water to the pot and poured another. I watched a current affairs programme and heard Jennifer at the door. I went out to the hall; there was nobody there. Somebody had pushed an advertising leaflet through the letterbox. I went back to the television. With rush hour buses full, and as Jennifer liked to walk, I guessed she was walking out from town. At the end of the programme I went out to the street where boys were playing football using the gate pillars of the house opposite as a goal. I stood for a while and watched them expecting to see Jennifer any minute. There was no sign so I went upstairs to get ready.

I was entirely alone, but being attached to a house on one side and only a few feet from one on the other I was conscious of people all around me. I pulled down the blind and turned on the shower in the bathroom. Like the television channels, a shower was a novelty; not standard issue in country rectories. I left the bathroom door ajar. When I got back to the bedroom it was half past seven, and I began to fear the worst. Either there had been an accident or Jennifer had gone for a drink. The odds were heavily on the latter.

I dressed and went downstairs still hopeful that she would be back in time. I couldn't concentrate on the television and went to the kitchen to tidy up. I went out to the front door again. The footballers had gone and there was a man cutting the strip of grass on the path in front of his house with a push mower. It was five to eight. I began to speculate about which pub in town she might be in, on the assumption that she was still in the centre of the city. The doorbell rang at five past eight. Heather stood on the step impeccably groomed so that I felt uncomfortably casual.

'Heather, how lovely to see you. I'm afraid you'll have to come in; Jennifer went to the Gallery this afternoon and she isn't back yet.'

Heather went back to the large black Volvo car parked at the gate and they both came in. If Heather made me feel uncomfortably casual Derek made me feel positively dowdy. He wore an off-white linen suit, a pink shirt, a club tie and fine Italian shoes, none of which items of sartorial elegance had I ever possessed.

'I'm sorry about this,' I said.

'Don't worry on our account,' Heather said, 'but what do you think has happened?'

My immediate instinct was to protect Jennifer, but I felt I could tell old friends, especially since we didn't see them often.

'I don't know if you've ever suspected, but Jennifer has a drink problem. She's an alcoholic, and I expect she is in a pub somewhere.'

Without responding to what I said Derek asked in a matter of fact way:

'What would you like to do?'

'She may come in any minute, or she may be late. I think we should wait a little longer and see. I have no idea where I might look for her. Do sit down.'

'Well, it's good to see you,' Derek said, 'I can't think when the last time was. It must be three years.'

'I've seen Jennifer in the meantime,' Heather said, 'but it must be at least that since we've seen you.'

'How is the parish?' Derek asked, 'and that beautiful rectory. It's got such character. What I'd give to live in a house like it.'

'It's a fine house, but in poor condition,' I said.

'That adds to its charm.'

'It does,' Heather said perceptively, 'if you don't have to live in it.'

I watched the clock, preoccupied with what I would do if Jennifer didn't turn up, not just for the meal, but into the small hours.

'Jennifer has had a problem with drink for some time, but this is the first time she has drunk on this holiday.' They were both uncomfortable with my directness.

'Are you sure she's an alcoholic?' Heather asked.

'I'm certain.'

Derek sat on the sofa with his arm along the back, exuding confidence and success.

'Well then don't you need to get her to Alcoholics Anonymous?' he asked, as though it was as easy as moving a junior clerk from one department to another. I tried to explain to Derek why it wasn't that easy, but realised he hadn't the remotest idea what was involved. He laboured under the classic misconception of the successful man, that the only thing lacking where people don't succeed is the kind of determination that got him where he is. This is based on the mistaken belief that all human temperaments and capacities are basically the same, and the only distinction between people is differences in motivation.

I gave them an outline of what was involved with Jennifer and her drinking, and Heather, embarrassed at Derek's lack of awareness, said:

'You see it's not as simple as it appears,' and then to me: 'It must be difficult for you in the parish.'

'I'm past that stage. I've learned there's nothing I can do. At one level I no longer care what anybody thinks, but I still protect her from gossip when I can. All I can do is wait until she comes to her own acceptance of the problem and that could be a long way off.'

As I talked to Derek and Heather I realised that, apart from Kate, I had never discussed Jennifer's drinking with anyone.

'The hardest thing is enduring her anger and rejection when I react to her drinking, and sometimes even when I don't. What keeps me going is the hope for a new life for both of us when she's dry. My great fear, however, is that she will damage her health before that happens.' Not wanting them to have to say anything in response I said quickly: 'We'll have one drink, and if she isn't here we'll leave a note.'

I was torn between hoping Jennifer would arrive in a fit state to go to a restaurant and the fear that she would arrive drunk and insist on coming. The table was booked and there was no reason why the rest of us shouldn't have our meal. We finished our drinks and I wrote a note to say we wouldn't be late. I was sure at this stage that she wouldn't be in until all hours, but I worried that she was out of her routine and, being under the influence, she would be vulnerable in the city.

We arrived at the restaurant where Derek was obviously well-known. It was the kind of restaurant that, first as a student and then as a cleric, was way out of my league. It had plush carpet, low lights, white linen tablecloths, a pretentious array of cutlery and glass. A waiter with an obsequious demeanour showed us to our table and lit the candle with a cigarette lighter from his waistcoat pocket. We were late, so Derek decided we would dispense with a pre-prandial. We each examined the menu and Derek and Heather had a knowing conversation about what was on tonight and what wasn't. Derek snapped his menu closed before I had even come to terms with the layout. I chose quickly without reading the whole list, in order not to betray my unfamiliarity with a menu of such ostentation.

At first I found conversation a strain because Derek and Heather were really Jennifer's friends and they didn't know what to say about Jennifer and her problem. They made what they thought were helpful suggestions that confirmed that neither of them had an idea of the real nature of the problem. I thought that I knew something about it, but they knew nothing. I tried to steer the conversation onto their interests and to general topics, but they kept coming back to Jennifer. They couldn't quite grasp that I had become used to it; that life must go on and that there was nothing I could do but wait.

Despite all this we had a pleasant meal. The food was good and two bottles of wine between us oiled the wheels of conversation, and there was the inevitable reminiscing about college days; who married who, and where everybody was now. There were even a few dead. Conscious of Jennifer we didn't sit on long and arrived back to the house about eleven. I pressed Derek and Heather to come in; I felt they had to see Jennifer no matter what state she was in. I went ahead of them through the hall into the sitting room. She was back. She was asleep, dishevelled, on the sofa and clearly drunk. I was glad that Derek and Heather would see her in this state to bear the reality in on them. I would protect Jennifer from parishioners, but it was no harm that friends should know, especially Derek who in his omniscience had an answer for everything.

I roused her. She sat up and took a moment or two to focus.

'You missed an excellent meal,' I said.

'Hello, Jenny,' Heather said.

Jennifer stood up and the two women embraced. They held each other tightly for a few moments and exchanged the mutual warmth of old female friends. They then stood at arms length and looked at each other. Jennifer's eyes filled up.

'I'm sorry Heather, please forgive me,' she said, tears running down her cheeks. Heather drew her in, hugged her again and said gently:

'That's all right. We missed you.' Jennifer kissed Derek on both cheeks and said:

'I'm sorry to mess up your evening.'

The three sat down and I went to the kitchen to make coffee. I could hear their conversation. Jennifer enquired for Derek and Heather's two daughters, both of whom had married suitably. Despite slurring slightly she was able to make conversation. Alone in the kitchen, unaccountably I was overcome by a feeling of tenderness for Jennifer. There was a sense in which I was immensely proud of her. Not for what she had done this evening, but for the beautiful person she was, for her honesty and her humanity that in recent times had disappeared beneath a myriad of obsessive and devious strategies to keep open lines of access to alcohol. Painful as it was for me to stand by helplessly and watch, and for Jennifer to be a slave to addiction, in a strange way we lived in the real world compared to Derek and Heather. I didn't think that we were necessarily making a success of it, but there was no denying it was real.

They went on exotic holidays, both played golf and Derek sailed. Why wouldn't they? They were both well-qualified, good at their jobs and worked hard. They were entitled to what they had; the house they lived in, the cars they drove and the clothes they wore. We lived in somebody else's house, drove an upmarket banger and often took clothes sent in for a jumble sale and put a few pounds in the kitty. I knew I didn't want their lifestyle, but maybe that was because I didn't have the option. I couldn't work out if my attitude was sour grapes that Jennifer and I could never be in their league and that I was simply making a virtue of necessity. Derek and Heather gave the impression that they had engaged with life and had succeeded, but it seemed to me that all the things that were important to them were designed to avoid the real human dilemmas of living rather than to engage with them. I knew from the experience of years working in parishes, however, that despite appearances, the old Chinese proverb was true which says: "No family can hang out a sign; 'nothing the matter here.'"

I brought in the coffee and poured it.

'And how is biz?' Jennifer asked Derek, 'not that I know the first thing about it.'

'Keeping the head above water. It's hard to do much more these days.'

We drank the coffee and Jennifer sobered up slowly. We sat talking for an hour or more covering again much of the ground we had covered in the restaurant and Derek and Heather left with the inevitable resolution that we mustn't leave it so long to the next time. I took the tray to the kitchen, and Jennifer followed.

'I'm sorry. Please don't be cross. I'm terribly, terribly sorry.' I hugged her and held her.

'I'm not cross.' I said, 'I love you.'

She began to sob. We went back into the sitting room and sat on the sofa. It was not the time for me to mention her drinking, but I hoped she might be struggling with it herself. I held her hand and felt a warmth for her that had been suppressed for a long time. I watched the involuntary rhythm of her sobbing, and gave her my handkerchief. Slowly the sobbing stopped and she looked me straight in the eye for the first time for a long time and said simply:

'Thank you.' There was then a long silence between us that Jennifer ended with: 'It's late. We should go to bed.'

Jennifer did not drink again during the holiday. We arrived home both feeling better, but it was only a matter of days before her old routine became established again, then slowly it became worse than ever and we led again our almost separate lives.

CHAPTER 10

August was warm and sunny. It was ideal weather for harvesting the winter wheat, and many parishioners were up to their eyes in the harvest one way or another. Other than Sundays, there was little happening in the parish apart from the re-decoration of the church. The gutters, downpipes and roof repairs had been done while I was away, but I was determined that I would be there to oversee the inside painting. With Jennifer's help I had picked the colours, which was a case of finding the nearest colours to the old ones as possible.

Mr Armstrong had commissioned the painter, who once he had started was content to take instructions from me. Mr Armstrong went in from time to time and expressed himself satisfied with the job and didn't interfere. To my surprise when it was finished, he asked me if I was happy before he paid the bill.

After the painter had left, a work party of women moved in to scrub and clean the church from top to bottom. They had already had the hassocks re-covered and had the carpet from the aisle cleaned. A party of the men did a major clean-up on the churchyard. I had to admit that if it achieved nothing else, marking the anniversary gave the church a much-needed facelift that in itself was a good thing.

Most of the men would not be available until the end of September, after the harvesting of the spring corn, and even then some of them would be into the beet campaign. As far as the harvest was concerned Mr Armstrong was a gentleman of leisure, not because he had someone to do it for him, but because he had no corn to cut. He had only the curtilage, a small amount of woodland and forty or fifty acres on which he kept a few cattle and some sheep. Having paid a man to look after them there couldn't have been much in it for himself. Intelligence from one or two of the locals who had access to the house for one reason or another, was that paintings and pieces of furniture were disappearing slowly. This was almost certainly to the salerooms in order to ensure that the last of the Armstrongs could survive, and in due course expire, in his ancestral home. In the meantime he would create quite a stir with the festival for the church anniversary. As long as he was alive the local community would not forget the Armstrong name.

Despite my own reservations about the whole thing I was prepared to support the event. If it didn't have much significance as a celebration in itself, it would, as Jennifer and some of the parishioners said, create a bit of a stir and make for a bit of life around the place. Those who took the lead in planning and promoting it saw it as a flag-waving exercise.

The principal teacher agreed that when the new term started in September she would get the children to do paintings, make posters and rehearse a play. The bishop, most of the neighbouring clergy and the two local Catholic clergy had accepted invitations to the centrepiece of the celebrations: the service followed by a buffet meal in the parish hall. For some reason the presence of the bishop and a clutter of clergy parading at a service impresses people; clergy robed seem to add weight to the proceedings.

Shortly after we returned from holiday Jennifer had come in one afternoon:

'I need some money to pay the grocer.'

'How much do you owe him?'

'I don't know. I need to pay something off the account.'

'I'll pay him.'

'You don't trust me,' she screamed and stormed out of the room.

I discovered that our debt in the local grocery shop was now serious money. I don't know if Martin ever approached Jennifer about it before, but he continued to give her credit. I was embarrassed and Martin, whom I knew well, never said anything to me. The bank manager phoned me one day to say that Jennifer had approached him about a loan, but since our account was joint he couldn't do it without both signatures.

Jennifer had always walked home from the village when the pub eventually closed, but recently somebody left her home by car much later than usual. I never questioned her about who she had been with or where she had been. To have done so would have aggravated the tension at home, led to more conflict and it wouldn't have achieved anything. She had always been up at some stage for breakfast, if only in her dressing-gown, but now she stayed in bed some mornings until after noon when it was time to prepare the mid-day meal. She had stopped doing other housework, and I found myself cleaning and tidying to keep the place barely respectable, especially when I knew parishioners were coming to the rectory. Things were peaceful enough between us as long as I said nothing about her drinking. This meant that our lives that had intersected briefly on holiday were lived in parallel again and moved even further and further apart.

Jennifer looked wretched. Now that things were getting steadily worse, I found myself for the first time depressed at the prospect of her not being able to stop. I knew that if she did make the break, she had the grit to stay off it. In fact I could imagine her, given her temperament and with the zeal of the newly converted, campaigning against drink in as all-consuming a way as she now indulged in it.

Until now the only person locally I had talked to about Jennifer was Kate. Despite being particularly friendly with a few parishioners I felt to talk to them would be disloyal. I could only speculate that different kinds of parishioner had different attitudes to the drinking habits of the rector's wife. I had no doubt that a fair number saw it as letting them down in the face of 'the other side.' The truth was that many of them saw their religious identity as simply not doing or being what Roman Catholics did or were. This did not necessarily mean that they were anti-Roman Catholic or hadn't got a respect for their Catholic friends and neighbours, but that any attempt they might make to define themselves religiously they couched mainly in terms of contradistinction to Roman Catholicism. They might even think that Catholics might use a wayward clergy wife as justification for clerical celibacy. I had no doubt that there were a number of parishioners who had sympathy for me and for Jennifer, and others who saw it as simply a moral issue deserving condemnation.

I called from time to time to Kate, who by now knew the full extent of the problem. All I wanted to do was talk, and Kate was a good listener. She was coming to terms with her own situation, and she understood mine. She listened with an understanding that was part of her gentle nature, yet she was realistic and strong. I understood more and more why she and Jennifer got on so well, however, recently Jennifer had not been calling to Kate, and now that school had started again Kate was less often at home. On one of my visits, largely out of curiosity, I asked Kate what the attitude of people in the village was to the rector's wife in the pub drinking and getting drunk. According to Kate, the publican and patrons were surprised when Jennifer began to frequent the pub, but she soon put them at their ease with her friendliness and matter-of-fact attitude to everything. As her drinking became worse some of them became protective of her and Kate knew that many of them had sympathy for me in my position. Kate was aware that things were getting worse and somebody had said to her recently that they were afraid that Jennifer might be knocked down on the road on the way home. I was long since past caring what anybody thought of Jennifer's drinking. All I cared about was that she would soon come to herself and be able to stop.

The work for the approaching anniversary event kept me from dwelling too much on Jennifer and her problem. The harvest was over and after the Harvest Thanksgiving Service the whole focus was on the festival. The subcommittee had done their work well and there was good support from the parish and the village. As the time approached there was even an air of anticipation, and some of the parishioners had involved their Catholic friends to help. The whole thing was meat and drink to Mrs Bowers who had eased herself back into things in time to decorate the baptistery in the church for the Harvest Thanksgiving. She was still not on speaking terms with Bob, who wasn't backward in confessing that he wasn't a bit sorry, as when she was sulking it made life easier for him. She did everything to such a high standard that she made everyone else feel inadequate, which wasn't by chance; this was why she did it. She had an insatiable need to be the best, and she was prepared to do anything, including not-so-subtle denigration of others to achieve it. She was a good organiser, but the only way she could work with other people was to tell them what to do.

As is usual with so many things women took the leading role and did most of the work. Many of the men involved themselves only in so far as their wives roped them in. Ann and Valerie did the planning and organising and although Willie was a member of the sub-committee, as the time approached he seemed to fade from view. John was a willing pair of hands and worked to Ann and Valerie's plan getting others to help when necessary.

The primary school is the lifeblood of any community; its future is nurtured there. The theory is that the school is the nursery of the community, and it is true to say that where a school is closed the parish is deprived of a distinctive sense of the future, even for those who have no children themselves. The parish belongs to the parishioners, and while the role of the rector is essential, the individual rector is a transient being and as such cannot have the same investment in the school, or indeed in the future of the parish itself. This is true especially in the country where most families were there, in many cases for generations, before the rector arrived and will be there long after the rector is gone. Our own children didn't go to that school, and I felt that it 'belonged' to the teachers, the children and the parents and it was my role simply to help to support it.

The teachers mounted an art exhibition of the children's work and put on a play. Not only parishioners, but also people from the village went to these events and they had both been a great success. There had also been a performance by her pupils staged by the local Irish dancing teacher and an exhibition in the church of the handiwork of the local flower club. All of these occasions were a build-up to the main event of the festival: the service, followed by a sit-down supper in the hall.

On the evening before the much planned-for event I was sitting in my study. Jennifer, as usual, was out. There was a ring at the front door. When I opened it there stood a man I gauged to be in his early thirties. I didn't know him and my initial impression was that he wasn't local. This wasn't unusual; people I didn't know sometimes turned up at the rectory where they knew they would get a sympathetic hearing. He was casually dressed, of average height and spoke with an English accent.

'Are you John Wood?' he asked.

'I am.'

'Can I talk to you?'

'What is it about?' I asked, being cautious as clergy need to be with people they don't know who call to a rectory.

'It's very personal.'

'Come in.' I led the way to the study where I sat at my desk and invited the young man to sit in the armchair. He sat on the edge of the chair and appeared nervous.

'This will come as a shock to you, but I believe that you are my father.'

'There's some mistake; you've got the wrong man.'

'I don't think so.'

'In the 1950's did you work in a bank in College Green, Dublin?'

'I did,' I said, content that he had got the wrong bank clerk.

'Did you know a Maura Murray who worked there too?'

In an instant I was whipped back to my late teens and early twenties, my years in the bank. I hadn't thought of Maura for many years.

'I did.'

'Well, she was my mother.'

My stomach turned over and I became aware of my heart beating. My immediate thought was not for Jennifer but for Mary and Peter.

'You say, was your mother. Is she dead?'

'Yes, but she told me the story just before she died.'

By now I knew that there was a chance that he might be right. I asked him to tell me what his mother had told him.

'She told me that you went out together and that you were very fond of each other, but she was Catholic and you were Protestant and in those days that wasn't approved of. But that wasn't the reason she went away. You confided in her, as you had confided in nobody else, that you were thinking of going for the Church. She knew that if you did you couldn't marry a Catholic, and she didn't want to stand in your way. Then she discovered she was pregnant which she was sure would prevent you from becoming a clergyman, so she left the bank and went to England. I was born and when I was two years old she married my father; that is the man I knew all my life as my father.'

I cannot begin to recount the thoughts and feelings that assailed me. We sat in silence for what seemed an age. I went over in my mind what my life might have been.

'I'm sorry, I haven't asked your name.'

'John, John Miller. When my parents married I was given my father's name.'

'John, I certainly need a cup of coffee. I'll put on the kettle. Would you like tea or coffee?'

'Tea please.'

In the kitchen I went over in my mind those early years in a way I hadn't done in a long long time. Maura was a fine person, kind, gentle and wonderful fun. We went out together for well over a year. Apart from Jennifer, she was the only woman I had ever loved. I had never understood why she wanted to go to England. We corresponded for a while and then I too left the bank, to study for ordination. We lost touch and then in college I met Jennifer. All the implications of John being my son went through my head. Yes, I knew that he could be. If he weren't how could he know what he had already told me? Without knowing his exact age, the time scale made it possible. I brought the tea and coffee into the study.

'How did you find me?' I asked.

'From a Church directory. In the spring I was over to visit my mother's family in Dublin and came down. I drove up the avenue but couldn't bring myself to come to the door.'

Lots of things came into my head, but having asked John some questions the time scale was right and I dismissed them. What confirmed for me that he was my son was that everything he told me about his mother was entirely in character with the Maura that I knew and had once loved. I tried to see Maura in his appearance and couldn't; she was young when we went out together. I wondered if he was like me, but that is always for somebody else to see, and 'likeness' is often more in manner than appearance. We talked and talked for a long time exchanging information. He had left school early and had done a stint in the army. When he left the army he did different jobs; he seemed to be a bit of a rolling stone. He had recently lost his job as a storeman. He had had a broken marriage, but no children and was now living outside London with a partner. After about two hours together I was mentally and emotionally exhausted. Eventually John stood up:

'I must go, I have to get back to Dublin.'

'I have a lot to come to terms with,' I said. 'Please give me your address and I will write. You feel free to write to me too.' I led the way to the hall door. On the step John put out his hand. I took his hand, gently drew him to me and hugged him tightly. I felt it was the least I owed him. He was stiff and embarrassed. It felt as though he had never been hugged before, at least by a man. I walked him to his car and said:

'I look forward to hearing from you and I will write when I sort myself out.'

I waved as he drove down the avenue.

All the implications of what I had just learned raced through my mind, for myself, the children, Jennifer and for my job. I was sure that if I asked John to keep confidence nobody else need ever know. But I revised this when I remembered that he had given some information to his father and perhaps to his mother's family in Dublin. For most people a secret is telling only one person at a time.

I went back into the study and sat into the armchair. In the early days of our marriage, if I had known about John and told Jennifer she would have taken it in her stride. In fact she was likely to have said that I had some responsibility to support him. These days, however, I was sure that in one of her angry outbursts she would be vindictive and use it against me one way or another to force me to enable her drinking. I would not tell Mary or Peter unless I had to, and parishioners need never know. If they did, I was beyond caring what they thought. It would give Mrs Bowers more to think about than Bob and the flower jars and more for Ted Saunders to feel self righteous about than Jennifer's drinking and the shake in her hand. Maybe on my next visit Kathleen would let me in the back door and entertain me in the kitchen. I suddenly remembered the bishop and wondered what he would think. Might I have to offer my resignation? If it were accepted it would solve my recurrent uncertainty whether I should be in the job at all or not.

I knew it was possible that Maura and I could have conceived a child, but I began to realise that there were other ways than the one John recounted that a person could know. While initially accepting what he had said as true, as the days passed all kinds of doubts and combinations of possibilities crept into my mind. I settled for believing that Maura did have a child that in the circumstances was probably John, but why did he not look for his father before now?

The evening of the big service arrived and a large cross-section of the community packed into the church. The normally unused balcony was full to overflowing and creaked under the weight to the point I became seriously concerned that it might collapse onto the congregation below. A large number of people had to hear the service relayed to outside. The church itself looked well. Dampness in the walls hadn't had time to stain the new paint, and the words of Job, though in gold leaf and not graven, as was his aspiration, 'with an iron pen and lead in the rock for ever,' were emblazoned above the east window. They proclaimed: 'I Know That My Redeemer Liveth.' The flower arrangements of the flower club, if somewhat formal and lacking in imagination, added something to the occasion.

Robert Armstrong, along with the local TD, County Councillors and representatives of organisations in the village, sat importantly in reserved seats at the front. In the procession there was an assortment of clergy. Catholic priests in multi-buttoned soutanes with elaborately worked lace ends to their cottas, Church of Ireland clerics in cassock, surplice and black scarf with a variety of academic hoods and the sober-looking Methodist Minister, grey-suited with gown and white preaching bands. The procession was completed by the purple episcopal presence bringing up the rear, in red chimere and carrying a crozier taller than himself.

The form of service, including the words of the hymns, was provided on a service sheet, which enabled the Protestants to sing lustily and the Catholics to follow the words. Most of them weren't used to singing in church. Fr Keane and I read the lessons and the high point was the sermon preached by the bishop. He preached well, having done his research carefully. He outlined the political situation at the time the church was built, and contrasted it with the present to show how the spirit of reconciliation was abroad in the land. He acknowledged the Armstrong family connection and affirmed the whole-community dimension of the occasion. The rousing rendition of the last hymn 'Now thank we all our God,' was a fitting end to the service, which was more an affirmation of developing ecumenism than the celebration of the one hundred and fiftieth anniversary of the church or the Armstrong family's involvement in its building. The whole congregation poured out into the night and across to the parish hall for the speeches and for supper.

Jennifer was not in the church. She promised me she would not be late and that she would sit with the bishop's wife. She was not in the hall either. It was overcrowded; it contained virtually every parishioner except infants and the infirm, and as many again neighbourly and ecumenical Catholics. Every religious group has its bigots and I could think of one or two parishioners who would feel that to have Catholics in the church was one thing, but to have so many of 'them' in 'our' hall was another.

Eventually the platform party of VIPs was seated and I called on the bishop to speak. As he stood forward there was a bustle towards the back of the hall. He began:

'It gives me great pleasure to ……' and was interrupted by a commotion at the door.

'It gives me great pleasure to be here this evening…' he started again over the screech of chairs being moved on the wooden floor. Jennifer made her way up the side of the hall behind a helper making a passage for her through the crowd, to the steps at the side of the platform. At first I didn't recognised her. She was wearing her good red coat that hadn't had an outing for years, dark glasses and, unlike her, she wore a head-dress that was more feather than hat, from beneath which her recently cut hair pointed in all directions. As she got closer I saw that she was flushed. When she arrived at the foot of the steps she stopped, and holding the rail she looked up at the bishop, who by now was in full flight and ignoring the distraction. She stood listening and I hoped she would stay there until he had finished. After a minute, with a look that said, 'I'm not standing here any longer listening to this,' she pulled herself up the steps by the rail and onto the stage. She stumbled as she went around the end chair and made her way behind the second row to the vacant seat beside the bishop's wife. She pulled the chair back to get through, scraping it on the floor, pulled it into line and sat down. She turned to the bishop's wife and said in a stage whisper:

'I'm late.' The bishop's wife smiled a faint embarrassed smile.

With a great sense of relief that the interruption was over I turned my attention back to the bishop. He was in the middle of an amusing anecdote that I only half heard, at which everybody laughed heartily, relieving the tension and returning the atmosphere in the hall to normal. He ended by saying all the right things and thanking all the right people, including Robert Armstrong whose idea the whole thing was in the first place, and to whom I had at last conceded credit.

The bishop sat down, and while I waited for the applause to end, before I stood up Jennifer made for the microphone.

'I'm sorry I was late. Tonight of all nights I was held up.' Someone with a quick wit down the hall laughed out loud and smothered it. Jennifer hesitated and lost her train of thought. After an embarrassing silence she recovered and continued:

'The great thing about tonight is that everybody who's anybody is here. By this I mean not only you, bishop, but our local TD and County Councillors. They have all asked me to tell you that when you vote at the next election you are not to take into account that they took the trouble to come here tonight as they wouldn't want to gain unfair advantage over their opponents.' A few people laughed. Jennifer went on:

'Seriously, what's important is that the whole community is here. The days for making distinctions are gone,' and she slurred 'seriously' and 'distinctions' badly. I hoped that she was finished there, as in the circumstances she hadn't disgraced herself completely, but she stopped to draw breath and started again;

'So to parishioners I say; get up off your butts, stand on your feet and keep the show on the road or there won't be anyone left for our Catholic friends to be ecumenical with,' and she staggered 'ecumenical' two or three times. She steadied herself and turned towards her chair. I stood up quickly, but before I could step forward Jennifer swayed back to the microphone again. She took it in her hand and turning unsteadily to look at him directly, she said;

'And bishop, remember; Jesus wants you for a sunbeam.' She swayed back towards her seat again and sat down. For a moment there was silence and then some embarrassed applause around the hall. I stood forward quickly, thanked the bishop and said how particularly glad I was that Fr Keane had taken part in the service and called on him to speak.

Fr Keane was an especially kindly and generous-spirited man, of whom Jennifer was particularly fond. He said all the usual things in the circumstances, but he said them in his own kindly way so that you had no doubt they were not just a formality, but that he meant them. He said how much he agreed with the rector's wife about people coming together and that all traditions of the Christian faith had much to learn from each other.

When Fr Keane finished I thanked the vestry and the subcommittee for all their hard work and the ladies of the parish for the supper. I thanked Mr Armstrong for decorating the church and his contribution to the festivities, and called on the bishop to say grace. Then the women of the parish performed the miracle of the feeding of the multitude, but with a little more notice than Jesus had had in his day. During supper Jennifer engaged in animated conversation, largely one-sided, with the bishop's wife, but as time went on the less talkative she became. My only anxiety was that being one of those clergy wives with little time for bishops, she might be less than discreet, not because it might reflect on me, but her judgement about Church affairs were her own and she didn't pull her punches. By the time the bishop came to talk to her she had steadied up somewhat, and the two made polite conversation.

Despite my reservations beforehand I had to admit it was a good night. It was a notable occasion; not only that it had been a successful celebration of the hundred and fiftieth anniversary of the church, but also it was the night that Jennifer left nobody in any doubt that she had a problem.

CHAPTER 11

Shortly after John had called and before I had written, I received a letter from him. He said all the predictable things about having at last met his father. As he was out of work he wondered if I could lend him some money. My heart sank. All the thoughts that I had considered unworthy surfaced again, but this time with the possibility that they were credible. I was disappointed and decided not to answer the letter.

After the festival the parish settled into the routine of the winter season; all the bits and pieces that make up the social life of a country parish. The drama group was the only one in which Jennifer showed an interest. Despite having a mathematical mind she had an artistic bent, but it had been a couple of years since she had taken part.

Now that Jennifer had left nobody in any doubt that she was a drinker, I imagined there were fewer comments about her from parishioners. I used to wonder whether my sensitivity in the matter made me imagine that perfectly innocent comments or enquiries were prurient or snide. Though I didn't mind for myself, I felt for her that parishioners were gossiping and some of the holier-than-thou ones were judgemental. I had no doubt, however, that some parishioners were sympathetic to me having to live with the problem and to Jennifer as victim of it. I didn't know much about the condition, but the one thing that I did know was that it was much more than wilful badness, and that without help she would not be able to overcome it. I had always made the assumption that some parishioners felt that Jennifer was letting them down in the eyes of the broader community. My own experience, however, was that members of the Catholic community were far less likely to take the high moral ground on the issue of her drinking than Jennifer's co-religionists who themselves were less under scrutiny by the majority than they imagined. Though different religiously they were socially well accepted as part of the community at large.

Much of the time I was lonely and isolated, and when Jennifer and I did communicate, if it weren't purely formal, it was likely to be acrimonious, and I wanted to avoid that at all costs. At this time I was looking after almost everything; the shopping and housekeeping as well as the parish. When Jennifer was still doing the shopping she spent the bare minimum of money and kept the rest. She still hung on to preparing our mid-day meal.

She drank as much money as she could lay her hands on, and I had to ration money to her, which was the main cause of her anger towards me. She would plead with me and when either I didn't have any money or wouldn't give it to her she became abusive. She even suggested that I borrow from one of the parish accounts and she would pay it back. 'It would only be a loan,' she said. When I refused and made it plain that under no circumstances would I do that or anything of the sort she stormed off in a sulk. I suspected that the pub in the village had stopped giving her credit, as sometimes when I knew she had no money and I had none to give her she would stay in and go to bed early. I planned that when she stopped I would pay off her debts bit by bit.

I alternated between feeling sorry for Jennifer and feeling angry that she was creating hell for both of us. I wanted to help her but I could do nothing but stand by and watch her destroy herself slowly as she had destroyed our marriage. I was beginning to lose hope that she would ever stop drinking. She sometimes had a jaundiced look so that I was afraid she had done damage to her health. It was hard to believe that she could go on so long. Jennifer and I lived in the same house, but there was almost no communication between us.

I had stopped trying to talk to her about her problem, as it only made matters worse, until one morning in the kitchen after she had stayed at home the previous night. In a fit of frustration I couldn't resist the temptation to broach the subject on the grounds that there was nothing to lose.

'Jennifer, can we talk?'

'About what?'

'I want to tell you how I feel. I feel alone and afraid.'

'What are you afraid of?'

'I'm afraid because things aren't the same between us. When we talk at all, which isn't often, we end up arguing.'

'Well that's not my fault,' she said turning away to clear the table.

'It takes two to have an argument and you know there are two sides to every story.'

'So what are you saying?' she asked without turning around.

'I'm saying we should talk about it, so I can tell you how it's affecting me.'

'Talk about what?'

'You know very well about what.'

'I don't, tell me.'

'Your drinking.' She came back and sat at the table, and with mock patience she said:

'How many times do I have to tell you, my drinking is under control? I can stop when I like.'

'Well why don't you then?'

'I plan to soon, but it's all I have for company. You're not the only one that feels alone. You're out in the parish or you have meetings. Am I to sit at home on my own and twiddle my thumbs? Now that's an end to it. I don't want to discuss it any further.'

Ignoring her I said:

'You can't stop when you like, you're an alcoholic.' She looked daggers at me across the table and her face flushed to beetroot red.

'I told you before I'm not a fucking alcoholic,' she screamed at the top of her voice, leaning across the table, 'and what the hell would you know about it anyway?' She stood up, kicked back her stool, knocking it over, and stormed out of the kitchen slamming the door behind her.

I sat immersed in the silent alienation of the aftermath of her anger, and knew I should not have tried. I focused on the thought that had entered my mind from time to time recently: that I could no longer stay in the parish. Not because of what people thought, but because my faith and my life were in turmoil, and I had nothing to give to anybody any longer. I had begun to resent demands that parishioners made upon me; perfectly reasonable demands under normal circumstances, but demands that I couldn't cope with and that made me unreasonably angry. I wanted to get away from everything to do with the parish, and for the first time I admitted to myself I wanted to get away from Jennifer.

I sat stuck to the seat, staring out the window. The sky was a mass of black cloud and the wind drove sheets of rain across the garden. Not a leaf remained on the big beech tree and I could see through the gaps in the thorn hedge into the field where the cattle stood along the fence, heads lowered and backs to the driving rain. I wasn't angry. In fact I felt nothing; I was numb. I was cocooned in a world that included only the numbness inside my head and my view through the window, which by now had become largely occluded by the rain running down the glass making it almost opaque. As the rain eased a little I could see the beech distorted through the wet glass. Slowly my mind began to work again and since I no longer believed in a God that intervened, I began to take the hint of comfort from the possibility of leaving; I felt the absence of God, which I experienced as the absence of love. Those who formerly loved me had moved away; Jennifer into her own alcohol-obsessed world and the children, rightly so, each into their own world and for whom I was no longer a present reality.

I cleared the table and went out into the hall. I stood at the foot of the stairs and called Jennifer; there was no reply. I called again, and then went up to the bedroom; she wasn't there. I came down and checked the downstairs rooms. No sign. Her coat was gone, but even with a coat she would be drenched. I went into the study and sat at my desk. The wind was gusting at force and driving rain across the avenue. I took my coat and got into the car, and half way to the village I found her sheltering under some trees, wet through. She got in beside me without a word and I began to turn the car on the road.

'Where the hell are you going?'

'Home, to get you dried out.'

'Stop,' she shouted, 'I'm not going home, I'm going to the village.'

'You're wringing wet. You can go to the village when you've changed.'

'I'll make my own decisions. Stop the car. I'm going to the village.' As I drove back to the rectory she screamed and began to punch me on the head and on my shoulders. As I tried to avoid her blows the car swerved onto the soft verge and stalled. Jennifer tried to open her door, but I got going again before she could get out.

'You'll cause an accident. I can't make you change your clothes, but I'm taking you home and if you decide not to, that's your decision.'

In uncontrolled anger she beat the dashboard with her fists, and then put her head in her hands and cried with rage.

When we arrived home she got out of the car without a word and stormed upstairs. I went into the study and felt some satisfaction that for once I had stood up to her, but at a price. I knew I couldn't make a campaign of standing up to her at the cost of her rage. The sky brightened and shafts of sunlight poked through the clouds. I sat at my desk and listened. I could hear her at the hot-press on the landing getting some dry clothes. In a few minutes she came downstairs, went out through the kitchen and slammed the door behind her.

In the small hours of the morning she came home more drunk than I had ever seen her. I didn't always waken fully when she came to bed, but I had developed a sense of when she was in. She sometimes fell asleep in the chair in the kitchen, but woke and came to bed, usually by about three o'clock at the latest. That morning I woke to a noise on the landing and sat up in bed. There was a fumbling at the door handle. The door opened and Jennifer fell into the room, saving herself from falling onto the floor by holding on to the door. She steadied herself and closed the door. As she began to move across the room I turned on my bedside light. She put her hands up to shield her eyes and fell onto the end of the bed.

'Are you all right?' I asked.

She mumbled something, but did not move. I got out of bed and turned her onto her side. She was very drunk. I was trying to decide whether to leave her or put her to bed when she got violently sick onto the floor and fell off the bed onto her vomit. She lay there and groaned and began to heave again. I ran to the bathroom to get a towel and when I got back she had been sick again and lay on the floor, comatose. I put on the ceiling light and went to the hot-press to find a sheet. When I got back she hadn't moved. I spread the sheet on the bed and lifted her onto it. Her emaciated body was skin and bone. I got soap and a basin of warm water, undressed her, washed the vomit from her face and hair and put her into bed.

I cleaned the carpet as best I could, lay in bed and turned out the light. The smell of alcohol, which I was used to, was compounded by the smell of vomit. I couldn't sleep and turned on the light. I tried to read but couldn't. I became more and more angry for what Jennifer was doing to herself and to me, and all I could salvage from the situation was that the children had gone and were spared all of this. I could see no light at the end of the tunnel as I listened to her breathing, and in a moment of despair I wished that it would stop. I suddenly became acutely aware that I needed help as much as Jennifer, and made up my mind to find it in the morning. Who does the helper turn to when he needs help? In theory for me it should have been the bishop, *pastor pastorum*, but if I had gone to him and Jennifer had found out she would be apoplectic, and anyway he could do no more than pass me on to someone else. He could pray about it, and probably would, but at my stage of theological disintegration I didn't believe that that would do any good. I decided to start with our GP who knew us well and had my confidence. I tried to read again, failed, turned out the light and eventually fell asleep.

Next morning was the same as any other morning after Jennifer had been out the night before. I got up at my usual time and Jennifer arrived down to the kitchen late in the morning in her dressing-gown. She was her normal self and showed no more than the predictable effects of the previous night. I made a comment about her having been sick which she ignored. We had our usual intermittent conversation about nothing of importance, unless my plans for the day could be deemed important. These stilted conversations were occasions of mutually contrived stand-off.

I left her in the kitchen and went to the study. During the small hours, when darkness had cast a black veil over every thought, I had determined that I would phone the doctor. With daylight the veil lifted and now I wasn't sure. Perhaps last night had been an exception provoked by me trying to get Jennifer to talk; maybe I would call to Kate, where I knew I would be well received, and offload to her.

On the spur of the moment I picked up the telephone and phoned the doctor and made an appointment for later in the week. As soon as I put down the phone I began to feel foolish; that he wasn't the person to talk to; that for ethical reasons he couldn't discuss Jennifer with me; that as an experienced pastor I ought to have been able to sort it out for myself. I kept reminding myself of the events in the middle of the night, and my feeling then that I needed a doctor as much as Jennifer did. In the days approaching the appointment I rehearsed many times how I would broach the subject, how I would begin in such a way that I would not feel foolish and that the doctor would take me seriously.

Up to the time I arrived for the appointment I was still uncertain what I would say. I wasn't clear in my own mind whether I was there about Jennifer or about me. The waiting room was full which convinced me that I was wasting the doctor's time. I had no doubt that all these people needed him more than I did. I sat looking at a copy of 'Cosmopolitan' without seeing it. When the receptionist called my name I felt butterflies in my stomach. The doctor greeted me warmly with:

'It's funny you should come today; I was going to contact you about Jennifer. She's been to see me and her liver function is not good, but she won't agree to go for tests. I am not sure she's being very rational at the moment so I think it is in her best interest to let you know, so that maybe you could get her somehow to tell you herself and that you could encourage her to go.'

'What does it mean?' I asked.

'It will get worse if she doesn't do something about it. It should be investigated.'

'And if she does have tests?'

'We can start to treat her.'

'You know of course what the real problem is?' I ventured.

'Yes, I do. I tried to raise it indirectly, but I couldn't get her to talk about it. I tried a second time, but she got up to go.'

'To be honest with you,' I said, 'I think I need help. I feel I'm falling apart and don't know how to hold on. Jennifer's drinking is wreaking havoc on me as well as on herself; we might as well be living in separate houses. In fact it would be better if we were.'

'Sit up there,' he said ''til I check you over.' He examined me thoroughly, and declared there was nothing wrong physically, then added:

'What you need is to talk to somebody who understands the problem,' and he wrote me a note to a psychiatrist who specialised in alcoholism and he gave me a prescription for something to relax me. I left the surgery feeling better; I had talked to a professional, he took me seriously and there was something to be done. My immediate concern, however, was to get Jennifer to go for tests without revealing what the doctor had told me. It gave me some hope that if she went for treatment he would put it to her frankly that her drinking would damage her liver irreparably. Her capacity for denial, however, didn't encourage me that she would go.

Slowly a glimmer of hope returned, and I wanted to share it with Kate. I always felt I needed a reason to call to her and I hadn't been there recently because our conversations had been going over the same ground again and again and getting nowhere. I was afraid I was becoming a nuisance, though Kate was never other than her kind, cheerful self with her good sense of humour. Jennifer had all these attributes too, but for her they were subsumed under her obsession, so that I hadn't seen them for a long time. I had no doubt that nowadays she was two different people: her interesting affable self when out with her drinking companions, and irritable and volatile at home – street-angel, house-devil.

'Jennifer hasn't been here for ages,' was the first thing Kate said when I arrived. 'I phoned a couple of times and she said she'd call, but never did.'

'She sees nobody these days. She does nothing but drink and sleep and the bare essentials of housework. As far as I can see the only thing that keeps her at home at all is when her money runs out.'

Kate had an innate sympathy with human frailty. She didn't make judgements about people, even about Conor and Betty, but rather she was puzzled by significant human failings. Maybe it was her training in child psychology as a teacher or maybe it was simply her non-judgemental nature or a bit of both. Her instinct was to ask questions rather than make statements, and I was never sure what conclusions she came to, if any. Yet behind what might be interpreted as uncertainty or indecision there was a strong person with a sense of the right thing to do and the courage, often against the common consensus and conventional wisdom, to do it. She asked the right questions when I showed confusion and guilt over Jennifer's drinking:

'Are you encouraging her to drink?'

'Of course I'm not.'

'Well why are you feeling guilty?'

'I'm sorry for her.'

'Why are you letting Jennifer's problem make you ill? One member of the family should stay well and at the moment that can't be Jennifer.'

Kate made me promise to make the appointment with the psychiatrist, and she agreed to call out to see Jennifer and see if she'd admit to having been to the doctor. I didn't like conniving with Kate against Jennifer, but we both had no doubt that in the end it could be for Jennifer's own good. I wasn't hopeful, but it was worth a try.

CHAPTER 12

After I had seen the doctor I became aware that I was doing no more than the bare minimum in the parish. Conducting services on Sundays was almost unbearable. I kept them as short as possible and I got through by reading the words mechanically and doing something I had never done before; I read sermons from a book. I tried to put the sermons in my own words, but found I couldn't even do that. It was hard to concentrate to write even the simplest letter and I certainly didn't want to visit anybody. The truth was that I had lost interest in people and had become wrapped up in myself and obsessed with my anxiety for Jennifer. When talking to someone I said the minimum and couldn't wait to get away. I dreaded the ring of the telephone. I wanted to be left alone, and when I was alone I exhausted myself by going round in circles in my head. That's where I was trapped most of the time; in my head going round and round and not able to find a way out.

What was it that needed to happen before Jennifer hit this 'rock bottom' which people talked about that alcoholics need to hit before they will make a decision to stop drinking and find help? I felt she was already there and wondered how much worse it would become. Waiting for it to happen might be too late. It was a long time to next Lent when she would stop drinking, give her liver a chance and perhaps be more amenable to listening. I was sucked into her downward spiral and I had come to my own realisation that I needed help, but there was no sign of Jennifer doing the same. In fact she had become more dogged and truculent lately which indicated to me that she had no intention of changing anything. I even indulged in the mad fantasy of bringing her to some remote part of the world; to desert or tundra, up a mountain, anywhere where there was no alcohol. I wondered why she became an alcoholic and that I didn't; we both drank the same modest amount in the early days. Was it my fault that I had worked too hard in the parish and the 'devil had found time for idle hands'? I blamed myself, I blamed her and then I blamed the God I no longer believed in, for the God I did still believe in wouldn't be responsible for such a thing.

I oscillated between anger and pity. I hated her going out, knowing she would come home drunk. I dreaded the bedroom door opening and her falling into bed. Yet I was glad of the peace in the house when she did go out. For a long time I hadn't cared what people thought. Most people were too wrapped up in their own concerns to care about mine, and the wagging tongues, addicted to news, gossip and scandal, would move on to some other poor unfortunate individual in trouble when some fresh and spicier piece of gossip turned up. The kick goes out of gossip when the scandal becomes the norm. The bishop was the one person I thought should have been in touch with me. He had the perfect opening after Jennifer's performance on the night of the festival. I resented the fact that he hadn't, but I would not have received him well if he had. He was a good man in one way but harmless in another. He was academically good, politically astute and kindly, but when it came to people and their problems he didn't know his backside from the joint in his arm, and anyway he was the last person in the world that Jennifer would want me to talk to about her.

For three weeks I carried around in my pocket the prescription the doctor had given me, and I didn't make an appointment with the psychiatrist. When I did eventually have the prescription dispensed and took the pills I began to feel drowsy and fell asleep at the drop of a hat. I had to be careful in the car, and more than once I pulled in to the side of the road and went to sleep. I didn't tell Jennifer I was taking pills. She had no time for medicines especially for nervous or psychiatric complaints; she saw them as a sign of weakness. Ironically she thought that people with such complaints should be able, by willpower, to pull themselves together. Slowly the pills helped and I began to get things into perspective. I still did the minimum in the parish but didn't dread the phone or meeting people as much, and I disciplined myself to go for a long walk every day. I dropped into Kate more often. As well as listening to me talking about Jennifer, Kate talked about her own situation and the divorce that was almost complete.

I began to think seriously again about leaving the parish or even leaving the ministry altogether. I fantasised that a totally new situation would give us a fresh start. If Jennifer could get some kind of job she might have less time to drink, but I also knew that a change would bring a whole new set of problems and probably a new range of people for Jennifer to borrow money from. I knew that the only real option was for her to get help and stop drinking.

I began to pick up the threads of work in late November, and was just beginning to do more in the parish when I woke one morning just after four and Jennifer wasn't in. I sat up in bed, put on the light and checked the time on my watch. She often fell asleep in the kitchen but eventually came to bed. I put on my dressing-gown and went downstairs. She was not in the kitchen. Nothing had been disturbed since I had gone to bed. She had never been so late before. I began to speculate that she and her cronies had gone to one of the outlying pubs that stayed open as long as there were customers to drink, and perhaps they had had a puncture or a breakdown on the way back. I put on the kettle and made tea. In the stillness of the night it was just possible to hear cars on the road, and I knew that the cars that brought her home always dropped her at the gate. About half past four I heard a car. As it came closer I waited for it to slow down and stop, but it passed the gate and faded into the distance. When the same thing happened about half an hour later I began to be anxious. She might have been too drunk and may have gone to Kate to come home in the morning, but I dismissed that, as Kate would have phoned to let me know. By a quarter to six I was really worried. I oscillated between hope and fear and I reduced the possibilities of fear to the one I had always had, that she had been hit by a hit-and-run driver while walking home. For a moment my imagination ran riot and I started to panic. I was frightened and began to shiver. I turned up the cooker, boiled the kettle again and made another cup of tea.

I went back in my mind to before we were married, and how I had admired Jennifer's facility to think for herself. She had thought out most of the student issues of the day and she was ready to stand her ground against all-comers, while her friends were simply toeing the radical line. Not that she wasn't radical in most things, but she did not subscribe to anything simply because it was fashionable with her friends. Most of my contemporaries who were ordained met their wives through the student Christian groups at university or through choirs and parish organisations. I met Jennifer first on a student anti-nuclear protest. I was attracted to her intelligent commitment and felt she understood precisely why she was there. She wasn't there to do the student thing of protesting; she could give a host of reasons why the whole nuclear thing was a travesty of what civilised society and nations should be. Her conviction did not come from a Christian perspective, but from an uncomplicated view of what she understood it meant to be human. Her parents were tribal, non-churchgoing, rather than believing, Christians and she and her brother were sent to the local church and Sunday School until they were confirmed, shortly after which they too became non-churchgoing. After our first meeting I had admired her from a distance. Then came to know her as a friend long before I loved her, and by that time, to my surprise, she loved me too; a love that in recent years had been buried under a mountain of lies, anger and deceit. I remembered special moments together in our courtship and early marriage that were pure magic. Long walks in the hills, when there was still so much to discover about each other. I remembered how, on those long walks, I enjoyed her questioning mind; the freshness of her thought and the time we made love in the bracken. I remembered the times we were apart and the anticipation of being together again, and how in my first curacy she was determined to support me, without becoming 'a clergyman's wife,' and to this end on principle she would never drink sherry, and to my knowledge hadn't to this day. This was the love that, when she stopped drinking, I hoped beyond hope we would recover, but I was finding that hope harder and harder to sustain.

I decided to drive as far as the village. I went upstairs and pulled on trousers and sweater over my pyjamas. I put on a coat, scarf and shoes and took a torch. It had been raining recently and it was bitterly cold. I started the car, drove down the avenue and turned right onto the road, all the time hoping I would hear a car coming and see lights. I drove slowly and kept a close eye on the verge on both sides. If Jennifer had fallen into the ditch she would be wet through and especially with her body weight she would be suffering from hypothermia by now. Every possibility went through my mind: being hit by a car, falling into the ditch face down and drowning in shallow water, even being attacked and left unconscious. I stopped at points where I knew the ditch was deep to look down. When I arrived into the village there was only one light on the whole length of the street. There was the slightest hint of dawn in the sky, but there was still nobody about. I drove slowly out the far side and turned around and came back. The darkness accentuated my plight and I resented the unconcerned silence of the sleeping village. I turned off the road and up the lane to Kate's house and from the gate I saw the house was in darkness. I drove back home, scouring the verges of the road again. I hoped that she had been dropped from the other direction and would be there when I got back, and I didn't care in what condition. As I drove up the avenue the only lights were the ones I had left on outside the front door and in the hall. I turned towards the yard and there she was lying face down on the grass verge on the yard side of the gate pillar beside a fallen coping stone.

I jumped out of the car and shook her; she didn't move. She was soaked right through. I called her name; she made no sound. I turned her over on the grass and propped her up. Blood covered one side of her head and face and had run down her front. I laid her down again, took her wrist and, with difficulty, found a pulse. I sat her up again and shook her:

'Jen, it's me. Jen, Jen.' She didn't respond. I shouted again and smacked her face; still no response. I slid my hands underneath her and lifted her up. I couldn't believe how light she was. I carried her into the house and sat her propped up on the chaise-longue in the hall. I tried to rouse her again, without success. I phoned the doctor and didn't know what to do next. I watched her shallow breathing and felt her pulse again. She was a sorry sight; bloodied, bedraggled and wet through, and I suddenly knew what to do. I ran upstairs to the hot-press and pulled out an armful of blankets, took the stairs down two at a time and wrapped them round her as best I could. I smacked her face and called her name, to no avail. I opened the front door, left it ajar, and pulled the chaise-longue on the two back casters into the kitchen; the only warm room in the house. I dragged it over to the cooker and turned the temperature control up to maximum. I tried rousing her and then had a closer look at the wound on her head. I couldn't see it properly with the blood matted in her hair, but it was clear she had hit her head a severe blow on the fallen coping stone. As far as I could see the wound had stopped bleeding. I lifted the cooker lid and pulled across the kettle, for what purpose I wasn't sure. It was something to do while I waited and there was no harm having hot water available. I went back into the hall and out onto the steps. No sign of the doctor. Back in the kitchen Jennifer was a little warmer and I tried to rouse her again, but she did not respond. I thought of trying to clean her face but decided the doctor ought to see her as she was. I began to realise that we would have to go straight to hospital. After what seemed like an age the doctor arrived. I told him what had happened and he felt her pulse and lifted her eyelids.

'How long do you think she was lying there?'

'At least two hours, possibly more,' I said.

'I'll phone the hospital and then I'll take you.' When he came back from the hall I lifted Jennifer up and carried her out to the doctor's car. The wet had come through the blankets under her. The doctor laid her down carefully on one side on the back seat and drove to the County Hospital eight miles away. On the way he asked me some questions to make conversation, that weren't directly relevant to Jennifer's present state. I desperately wanted some reassurance from him but I knew he couldn't give any. In fact the only comment he made was not at all reassuring:

'I'm afraid her general state of health won't help.'

The doctor had the car heater turned up full. I kept looking back to see if there was any sign of Jennifer coming round. There wasn't.

At the hospital some night staff were waiting. They lifted Jennifer onto a trolley and wheeled her in. I went to follow them, but they asked me to wait. I sat on a chair in the passage while the GP talked to a young doctor, and then came over to me.

'What do you think?' I asked.

'I'm not really concerned about the head wound, but I suspect there may be internal bleeding, and she'll almost certainly have pneumonia.'

I thanked him for coming and he left. After a few minutes a nurse arrived and brought me into a small room where she made tea and poured me a cup. For the first time since I had found Jennifer I thought of the children.

Mary and Peter knew that Jennifer drank too much at times, but since Jennifer reckoned she didn't have a problem, and I protected them from it, they had no idea how bad things had become. They were both away and getting on with their lives and as far as I was concerned they had no responsibility for Jennifer and her drinking, and I saw no reason to worry them at this point if it weren't necessary. I decided to phone them both later in the day when I hoped Jennifer would have regained consciousness, and when I knew the full story. After the best part of an hour, and after I had gone out onto the passage a number of times, the nurse came to tell me they were bringing Jennifer up to a ward.

'Has she come round?'

'No,' she said, as gently as she could make the word sound, without elaborating. 'I'll come and tell you when you can come up.'

Whatever the damage, I was impatient to hear that Jennifer had regained consciousness. Apart from it being movement in the right direction, silly as it may sound, for Jennifer being unconscious didn't fit. I know it fits for nobody, but somehow I found it hard to imagine her not thinking. On the other hand I could imagine her saying:

'Don't be foolish, I've as much right to be unconscious as anybody else, and anyhow if that's what nature decrees for me in the circumstances then it is probably the best thing for my survival.' I comforted myself by remembering a man I knew who fell off a horse and regained consciousness after two weeks and ever since he was hale and hearty. I remembered Jennifer's liver problem and thought the accident might have been fortuitous, as they could investigate it and treat it while she was in hospital. I gave myself hope by believing that this might be the 'rock bottom' she had to hit before she would make up her mind to address her drinking. This thought gave me an unexpected lift as I waited for the nurse to bring me up to the ward to see her.

Eventually a nurse came and brought me along a passage, up in a lift and along a corridor off which were two large wards of patients, mostly sitting up in bed having breakfast. I followed the nurse to the end of the corridor and into the intensive care unit, a small ward with four beds, one of them curtained off. The other three patients were all connected to monitors or machines of some kind, and as the nurse pulled back the curtain to let me in I saw Jennifer was connected to a number of machines too. I barely recognised her for the large bandage that covered her head. She was lying on her back and I could see her face only from her eyebrows to her chin. She had been washed, and I noticed how small she looked in bed. One of her machines was either breathing for her or was registering her breathing; I didn't know which and didn't know the significance of it. The nurse smiled and stood back to let me in beside the bed. I took Jennifer's hand and stroked it; there was no response. One of the nurses gave me a chair, and I sat down and waited.

'I know you can't speculate, but do you think it will take long for her to come round?' I asked.

'We don't know. We will be doing more tests later to-day and we'll have to wait for those results for a fuller picture.'

After about twenty minutes of fitful conversation with the nurse, during which time she checked and adjusted some of the equipment, she pulled back the curtains and left me sitting beside the bed. Another nurse came and asked me if I would like some breakfast. I decided not, but that I would go home, wash, dress and come back as soon as possible.

I thanked the nurses and left the ward in a daze. I didn't countenance the possibility that Jennifer might not recover, but rather clung to the hope that this would be the turning point for her, forced on her by the accident rather than arrived at on her own account. I seemed to be the only one around the hospital that wasn't in a uniform of one kind or another, which made me conscious of the ends of my pyjamas sticking out the legs of my corduroy bags. I felt suddenly tired as I went down the stairs towards the front hall. I had just asked the porter at the desk to phone a taxi, when a sister appeared from nowhere to say one of the ambulance drivers would run me home. After a few minutes a driver arrived.

'Your reverence, we're at the side door,' and he led the way, making pleasant ordinary conversation. It was a fine bright morning as we drove along the Main Street. The town was beginning to stir; shops opening, people going about their daily business. I felt no part of the world; rather I was outside it looking in from a distance. After initial politeness the driver lapsed into silence and I was too tired to make conversation. I was content to cope with the whole business on my own and I dreaded the prospect of people enquiring for Jennifer.

When I got home I phoned Kate, who had already left for school, so I left a brief message on her answer-machine. I asked her to do nothing until I contacted her later in the day. I had a bath and dressed, had something to eat and then phoned both the children to tell them the situation, and promised to phone later when I had more news. Mary wanted to come immediately, but I persuaded her to wait until I phoned again in the afternoon or evening. As I was about to leave for the hospital the phone rang. I didn't answer it; I couldn't bring myself to talk to anybody.

When I got back to the hospital Jennifer had just come round and was complaining of her head. The nurse was reassuring her and in a few minutes the nurse left and I told Jennifer what had happened. She hadn't remembered a thing and questioned me in a barely audible voice asking for details of where exactly I had found her and at what time. The nurse came with a cup of tea and propped her up a little in bed. Jennifer closed her eyes in pain at the move and thanked the nurse.

'I phoned the children,' I said.

'You shouldn't have,' she said, barely able to get the words out, 'they'll worry, and I'll be all right.'

I took the cup of tea from the bed-table and offered her a sip, but she refused. Her eyelids began to droop. I said something else quickly, afraid she was drifting away. She opened her eyes:

'I feel rotten,' she said, and closed her eyes again. I sat and held her hand while she drifted in and out of sleep. The nurse beckoned me away and suggested I shouldn't stay too long, but to go and come back later in the day. I was glad to have direction, as I didn't know what to do for the best.

I went home, couldn't settle to anything and went back after lunch. There was no change. I went again in the early evening and Jennifer was much the same. The children arrived together and were shocked to see her. Mary came out onto the passage with me and wanted to know exactly what her Mum's condition was. I hadn't asked for detail as I knew it was a matter of waiting. Mary went back to the ward and on her insistence I asked one of the nurses exactly what Jennifer's condition was. She phoned for the doctor on duty who was young and responded to my questions honestly.

'She's had a severe blow to the head and we must be careful about the internal bleeding. She also has pneumonia for which we're treating her.'

Desperate for re-assurance to pass on to the children, and not wanting to give them too much detail I asked the doctor:

'How would you describe her condition?'

'It's serious, but she's not in immediate danger.'

I went back to the ward. Jennifer's eyes were closed and Mary and Peter were sitting on either side of the bed. I took Jennifer's hand and she opened her eyes.

'It's getting late; I think we should go.'

'Yes,' she said slowly, 'these two have a long journey.' We said our good-byes and left.

In the front hall we talked for a few minutes and I told them what the doctor had said. I had never discussed with them the fact that Jennifer was an alcoholic, but it was clear they knew. Mary, who had always been more distressed by her mother's drinking than Peter, was angry. She seemed to be aware of what I had had to cope with.

'I feel terrible seeing her in that condition, but it's hard to feel sympathy for her. It's self-inflicted. It's her own fault.'

'She can't help it,' Peter said, 'It's a disease.'

'That's a cop-out. Mum is about the most clear-headed and strong-minded person I know. Why can't she exercise her will to control her drinking and if she can't do that, give it up altogether?'

'Maybe she will now,' I said. 'Maybe this is it.' I didn't want to hear Mary and Peter arguing about their mother, and wanted them to go back to Dublin with some hope.

We said good-bye in the car park. As I drove towards home I couldn't face the prospect of the phone, so I drove to see Kate. She answered the door with the chain on and let me in. Siobhán was in bed asleep. She turned off the television and poured me a stiff drink, and had one herself. It wasn't until I sat down that I realised how exhausted and emotionally drained I was.

'I've been 'phoning on and off, but obviously you've been at the hospital.'

I told her what the doctor had said.

'I think she'll be all right, but they are keeping a close eye on her.'

With Kate there was no judgement and no side of any kind. In fact I felt a kind of worldly-wise acceptance and a security when I was with her.

After the drink Kate made coffee and we talked until I fell asleep. When I woke Kate was reading and brushed off my apologies with:

'You're exhausted, and I don't wonder.' In the hall after I had put on my coat that she held for me, I turned to thank her. She squeezed and held both my upper arms, looked me straight in the eye, and said:

'You're going through the mill, but it won't last for ever.' My eyes filled up but I felt no embarrassment.

I turned off the alarm clock and slept till morning. When I woke the room was bright. I looked at my watch; it was just nine o'clock. It was a long time since I had had such a good night's sleep. I pulled back the curtains to a fine sunny morning. The remnants of a heavy frost lingered in the shaded parts of the garden and I could see in the distance Dan Dunne's cows ambling back to the field after milking and was glad I didn't have to get up every morning to milk a herd of cows. There weren't many privileges with my job, but one was that you could sleep late when you felt the need, apart from Sundays of course. I phoned the hospital; there was no change. I decided to take advantage of the weather and go for a long walk, have an early lunch and then go to see Jennifer.

I had breakfast, took a stick and left from the back of the house along the path that led to the forestry entrance. There were two routes that I walked in the wood; I took the longer one that went through a deciduous area that let sunlight through onto the pathway. It was wet from the night's dew and frost and it was muddy in places. When I got to the far side of the wood I didn't want to turn back, so I took a dark narrow track up the hill through tall conifers. When I emerged into the sunlight towards the top, the air was crystal clear and cold, but I was warm from walking. On the hill away to my right I could see the symmetrical pattern of tree planting with firebreaks that looked like a row of postage stamps. I could just see the roof of the rectory beyond some trees at the bottom of the hill. I walked slowly on to the top and looked across the valley to the other side to a line of low hills with the plain beyond. It was said that from where I stood five counties could be seen, but something similar is said about every high point in the country, and I didn't know enough of the topography of the region to be able to check.

I never stood on the top of a hill or mountain without wondering if that was the kind of view, only more so, that people with a traditional view of God thought he had of the world. The only human activity I could see was away to my right where a farmer was ploughing the headland of a large field. My thoughts in free flow ranged over many things from Jennifer in her hospital bed in the town that I could just about see in the distance, to Mary and Peter at work in the city, to my breakfast dishes unwashed in the sink in the rectory below and the thing that had worried me most recently, John and especially his asking me for money. I was removed from all these things and the world was getting on without me. Looking down on the world I had a strong sensation of not wanting to return to it, for going down the hill again would mean taking on the responsibilities that had worn me out. I understood why Peter the apostle did not want to come down from the Mount of the Transfiguration.

I was cold from standing and eventually made my way down the hill and into the wood. I took the short route home, and as I opened the door the phone was ringing.

'This is John. Did you get my letter?'

'I did.'

'Well?'

'John, I have no money. My wife and I are deeply in debt.'

'Your name is good.'

'I can't, I haven't any money. We owe money everywhere.'

'I only want £100.'

'That's a lot of money to us. No,' I said, feeling under terrible pressure.

'Who did you tell about me?' I ignored the question.

'My wife is seriously ill in hospital and I have to go. I'll write,' and I put down the phone.

It rang again immediately. It was the hospital.

'We've been trying to get you; come right away.'

'Is something wrong?'

'We're anxious about your wife. Come immediately.'

I thanked the nurse, and went to the car. From the way she spoke I knew it was serious. Despite, or maybe it was because, my mind was consumed by what I would find I didn't seem to be able to drive fast. I was cocooned inside my head inside my car, and drove by reflex alone. The matron, a nun, was waiting at the door when I arrived and led the way upstairs.

'They have done all they can,' she said over her shoulder.

When we arrived the curtains were around Jennifer's bed. The matron looked immediately at the monitors and the nurse left.

'She's had a haemorrhage,' the matron said gently.

I stood to the side of the bed and took Jennifer's hand. I rubbed it and said:

'Jen, it's me.' One of the few things I remembered from pastoral training was to be careful what you say within range of an unconscious patient; they can sometimes still hear. I said it again, and the matron who was behind me pushed forward a chair and I sat down. I turned round to acknowledge it and she made a gesture that left me in no doubt about Jennifer's condition. I left the bedside and from the nurses' desk I phoned the children. A few minutes after I went back the matron left and the nurse returned. I sat and watched Jennifer's shallow breathing. Eventually the matron came back and suggested I might like to stretch my legs in the corridor and she would stay. I walked up and down a couple of times and went back. The matron insisted I sit down. I sat and watched, and lost track of time until Jennifer's breathing became irregular. She would stop breathing and after what seemed a long interval she would take a deep breath and start again. The matron went to the other side of the bed and took Jennifer's hand. Eventually there was a sound from her throat and the matron went down on her knees, made the sign of the cross and began to pray. Jennifer's breathing stopped and I waited for it to start again as it had done a number of times. It didn't. I watched her chest; it was perfectly still. I stood up and looked across at the matron, now on her feet, for confirmation. She nodded her head gently a couple of times, came around the bed, put her hand on my arm and said:

'God love you,' and left. I was too exhausted to cry.

Conscious that the staff were leaving me alone with Jennifer, I stood and watched her still, spare body. I touched her cheek and said:

'Good-bye, Jen.' I knew she wouldn't have wanted me to pray. I pushed through the curtain and thanked the nurse. She said nothing, but I appreciated her firm handshake. The matron had been called away and would be back shortly. I went out onto the passage to wait, and stood looking out a window into an area of outhouses where a man in dungarees was piling black sacks of rubbish onto a trailer. The matron returned and I thanked her for everything. I felt no pain and no grief, just an overweening sadness that Jennifer hadn't had a second chance.

CHAPTER 13

Rituals and customs are important to people at a time of death, especially in the country. People observe them often without knowing why. The purpose of some of them is to help people to express grief and cope with parting. People have some of them simply in order to conform; not wanting to be different; not wanting the neighbours to be able to say: 'Do you know what they did at the funeral?' The great deep down fear for many is that people might think they rushed the corpse out of the house or into the ground. Jennifer took scant account of what other people thought, so I was determined that her funeral would honour who she was and what she would want.

Jennifer did nothing simply because it was 'the done thing.' She had strong views about funerals, and sentimentality or tradition had no place in them. She liked to get straight to the heart of a matter; one of her expressions was 'the unvarnished truth,' so I couldn't help but arrange that her coffin should be of raw wood; it would have amused her. There would be no plastic grass or other cosmetic accoutrement around the grave, all of which she considered devices to sanitise death. The grave would be filled in while the mourners stood and watched. She had once said to me that there was nothing to bear in on people the reality of death like stones hopping off the coffin lid and the earth piling up on top of it. She had always expressed a preference to be cremated: 'it's like revolution, a matter of shortening the time scale,' and hoped it would be available when she died, but it wasn't.

Jennifer didn't believe in life after death, and years ago, when she was in the whole of her health, talking about funerals she told me that at her funeral there was to be 'none of this "joyful reunion in the heavenly places" nonsense.' If there was she said she would come back and haunt me! I asked two of my closest clerical friends, Brian and David, both of whom Jennifer liked, to take the service, so that we doctored it to avoid some of the things that were anathema to her, and to me. She always referred to bishops as 'poncing around the place,' unfairly, I thought, as not all of them did. She hated the idea of bishops appearing robed at the funerals of clergy, their families and the gentry. As far as she was concerned in life, unfortunately, people were not all equal, but in death they certainly were, and bishops at funerals were often no more than ornaments, which role many of them were not designed for. Jennifer often wondered whether a bishop's blessing was supposed to be more efficacious than that of one of the rank and file clergy. I had to explain this kind of thing, as diplomatically as I could, to the bishop and the archdeacon who understood and both came with their wives and sat in the congregation.

Mary and Tom, and Peter came down together after lunch the day Jennifer died and stayed until after the funeral. She had loved them to bits, and for someone with such radical views on so many things, she believed in an old-fashioned framework of discipline during their upbringing. Above all she taught them to think for themselves. None the less in retrospect she believed she had been a poor mother. On their first night home we talked into the small hours and both Mary and Peter cried often. They had had no idea how bad things had been during the last few years.

Over the two days before the funeral they received callers to the rectory, despite knowing almost nobody, apart from family, since they had left home before we moved to the parish. Helped by some of the women parishioners they made tea and served the usual funeral sandwiches and cakes to people who came to offer their sympathy, and they talked to them as best they could.

On the day of the funeral Peter drove Mary and Tom and me behind the hearse from the hospital, followed by members of Jennifer's family and mine. About quarter of a mile, or even more, from the village, parked cars lined both sides of the road. When we arrived at the church there was a large crowd of people standing outside; as many as would fill the church again a couple of times. We got out of the car and waited at the hearse. Over the years I had met and conducted many funerals, and now I was on the receiving end. People approached to shake hands and offer sympathy. Brian and David led the coffin into the church and we followed. The church was packed, and people were standing in the porch, at the back and part way up one side of the aisle. The harmonium droned some dreary voluntary while the undertaker positioned the coffin and placed our three bunches of cut flowers on it. Knowing it was Jennifer's wish I had put 'family flowers only' in the death notice in the paper, which death notice Jennifer had once told me should be 'like Broderick Crawford in Highway Patrol; "Just the facts ma'am, just the facts."' There was to be no beloved this or deeply regretted that. She believed that relationships and grief were private to family and not for publication in newspapers. There were some wreaths left in the hearse that people, who either hadn't seen the notice or believed they knew better, had sent. This was all part of my main concern; to do things as Jennifer would have wanted, or rather to avoid doing things she would have abhorred.

Mary was beside me and we shared a hymn sheet for the opening hymn. I had selected the hymns carefully to avoid what Jennifer frequently referred to as 'sentimental theological nonsense,' and added to this the need not to have any reference to life after death, it was a difficult task. During the service I was in a kind of limbo, observing in a detached way what was going on, until David started his address. I had no idea what he was going to say. He touched on all of Jennifer's finest qualities, and then went on to say that in recent years she had succumbed to an illness with which thousands of people in society struggle. Jennifer in her saner moments would have been glad that David had been honest and open and had not swept anything under the carpet. He recounted that there had been good times in the children's growing up years, and that she had been a good wife and mother and a support to me in my work.

Everything he said was true, not that Jennifer would have agreed with the complimentary bits. After the prayers we stood for the last hymn, Jennifer's favourite, 'O Love that wilt not let me go.' No more than a few words into the first line I choked on a spasm of emotion, and couldn't get out another word. I composed myself and tried again and still couldn't sing. I spent the rest of the hymn just following the words on the hymn sheet. The blessing, then we followed the coffin out into the churchyard, to the open grave and the mound of brown clay, just as the diggers had thrown it up.

The undertaker lowered the coffin into the grave and Brian said the prayers to the accompaniment of the usual hum of whispered conversation from the back of the crowd. When he had finished, the gravediggers shovelled the clay into the grave as we stood and watched until there was a neat oblong mound of earth upon which Peter, Mary and I placed our flowers. As soon as the robed clergy moved away there was an endless line of people queuing to offer sympathy with a handshake and the ritual 'sorry for your trouble.' I had often felt sorry for mourners standing in a cold churchyard after a burial, but now that I was on the receiving end this repeated expression of condolence was reassuring. There were many I didn't know, some of them friends of the gregarious Jennifer. One, a small middle-aged man who smelled strongly of drink, wearing a shabby grey overcoat with cap under his arm, leaving exposed a pale bald pate over a weather-beaten face, held my hand, pulled me towards him and said into my ear: 'She was a lady, she treated everyone equal.'

Chapter 14

In the days and weeks that followed the funeral I lived in a state of confused, and often conflicting, emotions. Christmas was approaching and it was one of Jennifer's worst times. She was now free of what must have been for her an unbearable torment, and I was free of the madness that went with it. No more the awful feeling when she went out at any time of day that she would come back drunk. It was an end to the lying awake in the small hours waiting for her to come home and no more the poisoned atmosphere of the long silence the following day. No more the foul humour on nights when there wasn't any money for her to go out, or her fury if I said anything that even implied criticism of her drinking. No more the lies, the anger and the slammed doors. This wasn't the real Jennifer, but a chimera that had slowly emerged from her addiction to alcohol, an addiction that had destroyed a very special human being.

During her last years, all of this had been so much the norm that now I found it hard to adjust. It was as though I needed the chaos of Jennifer and her drinking to give back purpose and normality to my life. But all my acquired responses to cope with that mad world, while waiting patiently for Jennifer to come to her senses, were no longer needed. I was like a ship going full steam ahead suddenly rammed into full astern, churning up water and going nowhere. In the early days after her death, apart from keeping up the essentials in the parish, I was unable to concentrate to do anything, unable to adjust to normality; I had become used to chaos and couldn't create order. I was in a vacuum finding it hard to know what was solid. No longer did I have to cover for Jennifer in order to hide her worst excesses from people. I no longer felt the judgement, real or imagined, of the pious and the self-righteous, but rather I felt support from some parishioners that they felt free to give me in my bereavement, which they might have considered intrusive or even prurient while Jennifer was alive.

I felt the inevitable regrets of the recently bereaved: if only I had moved the fallen coping stone off the grass verge. If only I had gone to look for her sooner. If only I had gone to the psychiatrist for help, and above all I developed an obsession that Jennifer's problem with drink had been my fault. She was highly intelligent, a good mathematician and if I had been other than a clergyman or even if I had been in city parishes, she would have had the opportunity to develop a career of her own. She would have had more stimulation, less time on her hands and might not have resorted to alcohol. So many times I had reassured bereaved people that feelings of guilt after a death are normal and that so much of what people feel guilty about is unreasonable. It was a case of 'physician, heal thyself,' and I found it hard to do.

When I was on my own I oscillated between pity and anger towards Jennifer. When I was angry I was overcome by recriminations towards her and then I would begin to feel badly that Jennifer was not able to defend herself. I would picture her spare emaciated body lying still in her coffin six feet under the earth and my hope snuffed out. I was capable of justifying my feelings of recrimination on the grounds that when she had had the opportunity she would lose her temper if I said anything that was even the slightest bit critical. When I felt angry towards her I felt guilt, and when I felt pity I felt that I had diminished her; she was the last person in the world that would want pity. I also went through periods of self-pity that ended with my own guilt that I couldn't know what it was like for Jennifer to deal with her demon. I flailed about in the turbulence of powerful currents so that at times I struggled to keep my head above water.

As the days and weeks passed the imbroglio of my confused emotions slowly became disentangled and my thoughts of Jennifer were more and more of the good times; of the distant past. I found myself doing more in the parish and I was less fearful of talking to parishioners. Through all of the worst days of Jennifer's drinking and since her death I hadn't had a good cry or breakdown. I had called often to Kate, who had come through her own 'bereavement.' No matter what form I was in she received me in her own kind and gentle way, put on the kettle and we would sit and talk. Good listeners have friends who want to talk. I was one such, but there was more to my visits to Kate than wanting to talk about my life with Jennifer. Even when Jennifer was alive I had always appreciated Kate as a rounded person of great human understanding and warmth, and I talked freely to her particularly because I knew that she would not divulge to another living soul anything that passed between us. I told her about John, about his letter and phone call. From what I said she used the word which I was reluctant to use. She was right: it had at least the appearance of blackmail.

'How do you feel about people knowing?'

'The way I feel at the moment, I don't give a damn what anybody knows, with one reservation. I don't want to hurt Mary and Peter, but I think they would quickly come to terms with it.'

Over the years I had postponed dealing with my own demon: my difficulties of belief in the traditional faith. I had always told myself I would do something about it when Jennifer had recovered, and now that I was free of coping with Jennifer's problem I had no excuse not to confront it. I talked to Kate about all of this, and she was particularly interested as she had stopped going to mass, but like myself she hadn't rejected belief completely. She recounted how what she believed, though not based entirely on Church teaching, had helped her through her loss and the significant change in her life. She was able to offer much more to me than I had ever given her.

I had no difficulty with the teaching of Jesus, it was the teaching of those who came after him that I found incredible. The doctrines of the Church contrived by fourth century theologians, under no little pressure from the civic authority, had to account in retrospect for who Jesus was and how he related to God the Father and the Holy Spirit, in order to make sense of their belief that he was divine. Such were my problems with all of the early doctrines that when I thought about them I struggled constantly to know whether I should be in the job at all or not. When I finally revealed to Kate the extent of my difficulties, she wasn't in the slightest shocked. She asked questions to be clear in her mind what I was saying and treated the whole thing in a matter-of-fact way. I explained to her how I tried to reconcile what I did believe with traditional statements of the Church's teaching, but that it didn't always fit.

Eventually I felt such a hypocrite, believing as I did and functioning in the parish week by week, I decided to talk to the bishop. He gave the appearance of being a man of strong faith, who if he doubted would see it as a defect that he had to remedy by spiritual exercise, rather than that there might be something in his doubt. He would not be shocked by doubt, but would see it as an opportunity to strengthen his faith. He was by nature slow and ponderous and combined a strong traditional belief system with an honest and open humanity, so that people liked him, but sometimes he wasn't much good to his clergy. I knew, however, that whatever transpired he would be kind and try to understand as best he could.

I was clear in my mind that, in conscience, I would have to let him know where I stood. If he said I would have to go, it would be with mixed feelings. I enjoyed the opportunity the parish gave me to work with people, and I would miss that, but I wouldn't miss having to deal with the Mrs Bowers and the Betty's-mother kind of parishioner. I would end up with a clear conscience but no job and nowhere to live. I had often thought I would like to be a night-watchman, sitting at the door of a little hut gazing into a red hot brazier, with Thermos flask and sandwiches and peace while the rest of the world slept. But then the night-watchman was an extinct species, and I was certain I did not want to be a security man in an armoured van with an Alsatian dog, a helmet and a truncheon.

I phoned to make an appointment with the bishop. On the agreed day I arrived at the palace, and thought of the stable, the carpenter's shop and the itinerant preacher with nowhere to lay his head, and reminded myself that this interview could well mean I would soon be in the same boat. I climbed the granite steps to the big front door with polished brass knocker and knob. I thought of Gilbert's Admiral Sir Joseph Porter KCB who 'as office boy to an attorney's firm' had 'polished up the handle on the big front door.' And had 'polished up the handle so carefully, that now I am the ruler of the Queen's navy.' Unlike the bishop whose apprenticeship had been: the son of a rectory, a degree in theology, a PhD and some parish experience.

I pressed the bell and heard it ringing in the distance. There was a female foot-fall on the tiled hall and the bishop's secretary opened the big heavy door a quarter way and looked out from behind it, holding on with both hands as though having opened it she was in danger of losing control of it. I stepped into the hall. Among the clergy there were various opinions of the bishop's secretary. Some of them were careful of what they said to her for fear she would pass it on to the bishop. One rector in particular, however, who had no time for the bishop, used to say terrible things to her about him, not caring if she passed them on or not, but certain, so appalling were they, that she didn't.

'Cold weather,' she said as she closed the door. I mumbled agreement and followed her to the big drawing room on the right of the hall.

'The bishop won't be long,' she said as she showed me in. I thanked her and she disappeared leaving me to wait. The room was well furnished with original things. There was an oriental carpet on the floor and a magnificent gilt mirror over the elaborate marble mantelpiece. Apart from a rectangular space marked off by two sofas at right angles at either end of the fireplace, the room was dotted with chairs some in groups, and most of them covered in chintz. There were portraits of bishops of earlier days, and a cheap photographic portrait of the last bishop in a reproduction gilt frame. The room was clean, tidy and unlived-in. It was damp and it was cold. There was a one bar electric fire, not plugged in, between the sofas where I sat and waited.

After about ten minutes there were voices in the hall followed by the sound of the front door closing. The bishop entered the drawing room. I stood up, and he crossed the room with his hand out.

'How good to see you: I'm glad you've come. I've been meaning to get in touch.'

I didn't respond. He led the way to his study on the far side of the hall that looked out onto a lawn with a sundial in the middle. A large bookcase covered one wall. On one shelf there were photographs of his family and of high points in his career; his consecration, and a Lambeth group. The bishop sat behind his desk and I sat on an easy-chair away from the desk on the other side. After the civilities and before I had time to say why I had come he asked:

'Well, how are things?' I had a strong urge to ask him which particular things he had in mind but didn't.

'I've come because ......'

'I couldn't believe the numbers at Jennifer's funeral,' he interrupted.

'She was gregarious; people liked her,' I said, 'she was as popular in the community as she was in the parish. She and Fr Keane got on particularly well.'

'Of course I realised on the night of the festival that there was a problem.'

I would like to have responded: 'Well why the hell did you choose to ignore it?' but didn't, as it would complicate what I had come about.

'I've come to tell you that I'm not sure if I ought to resign.'

'Oh come now,' he said, 'It's early days yet. Give yourself time.'

'It's not that,' I said, 'it's that I don't know if what I believe, or rather don't believe, allows me to stay in the ministry, or even in the Church anymore.'

'Oh, that's not an uncommon grief reaction.'

'It's nothing to do with Jennifer's death,' I said, 'it's something that's been building up for years.'

'What is it you don't believe?' he asked.

'For example, I don't believe in life after death.' I said bluntly, to focus his mind, but I saw no sign that the import of what I had said had penetrated his complacency.

'Oh, we all have difficulty with that from time to time.'

'I don't have difficulty with it,' I said, 'I simply don't believe in it.'

'And how can you be so certain?'

'I'm not certain there isn't life after death, but I'm certain I don't believe there is, and I have no difficulty saying that that doesn't mean there isn't. Nobody knows if there is life after death; many people believe there is, but I'm no longer one of them.'

'As you know, it is central to the Church's teaching,' the bishop said.

I felt like saying 'Why the devil do you think I'm here,' but didn't. With nothing to lose I asked him: 'Do you believe in life after death?'

'Of course I do,' he said, 'and as you say I don't know, but I believe.'

'Is that because you really believe, or because the Church teaches?' He ignored my question and asked:

'How do you feel about taking a funeral service? That's based on the Church's belief in the hereafter.'

'I feel a hypocrite, but I convince myself I'm expressing something on behalf of the community, from which I myself dissent.'

'I see,' he said, and I felt he could perfectly easily have said next: 'And what do you think of the price of butter?' so lightly was he taking what I was saying. It was clear to me at this point that I was wasting my time. He wasn't taking me seriously, and gave the impression that this was a friendly chat between two clerics rather than that it was a serious matter for me. At the end of the day I was going to have to make up my own mind what to do; nobody else could help me.

'Are there other things?' he asked.

'There are …,' and he interrupted again.

'How is your prayer life?'

'I haven't got a prayer life as such, at least not in the sense that I have a discipline and a routine …'

'Well, there's your problem,' he said triumphantly, sitting back in his chair, pleased as Punch that he had solved the matter. I knew then for certain that I was wasting my time.

'Bishop,' I said, 'I spend a lot of time praying in my own peculiar way, but it's not what you would recognise as a prayer life. Thinking that's the problem is simply asking me to sublimate my reason to my emotions, and that's a form of indoctrination. I'm not prepared to do that.'

'Say more,' he said, using a kind of shorthand that surprised me.

'Well, to make a point, I don't believe that God intervenes in the weather to provide good harvests in this prosperous part of the world while he leaves millions of people in the Third World to die of starvation for want of rain. Nor do I believe that God intervenes in anything else in the natural order. It seems to me that it is legitimate somehow to ask God for help to cope with things, but not to intervene to change them.'

'Miracles do happen.'

'Well, it's about time we had a miracle to feed the millions of starving people in the world,' I said, and stood up. 'I'm sorry for taking up your time, bishop. Thank you for seeing me.'

'I'll think about what you've been saying,' he said, 'and do come again if you think I can help. Have you had a break? Perhaps you should try to get away for a while. I can give you some help from one of the funds at my disposal.'

I was cross and regretted I had come, and did not respond. I was tempted to ask him if he had a fund for paying off the drinking debts of the alcoholic wives of clergy, but didn't. We walked out into the hall.

'How are the children?' he asked. Either he had never known or had forgotten their names. 'I spoke to them briefly at the funeral.'

'Fine, thank you,' I said and we shook hands and I left. He had closed the door before I was into the car.

I drove out onto the street, cross with myself that I had come. I could have predicted the outcome. I knew he would pray for me in his regular devotions, but nothing he had said had been any help. I drove out through the suburbs and the parishes of my colleagues, and wondered how they coped with the kind of problems that had me thinking that I should leave. Maybe it was the case that in the country I had too much time to think. The city clergy certainly worked hard, but it was too easy to let the organisation become an end in itself. I had never heard of a clergyman leave because he lost his faith, not that I had lost mine completely. As I did from time to time, I suddenly began to doubt myself. Maybe all the others had the same kind of questions that I had, but took them in their stride, as a natural part of believing, and got on with the job. Maybe I was making too much of my difficulties. The bishop obviously thought so, as there was no hint from him that I might have to give up if I went on like this. Why should I worry if it wasn't a problem for him? I had done everything I could.

Halfway home I pulled into a lay-by with a view across the valley to the mountains beyond. I didn't look forward, despite everything, to arriving back to the rectory where Jennifer would never be again. I felt relief, however, that I had spoken to the bishop, for in recent years I had somehow tied the two things together, Jennifer's drinking and my doubting, in such a way that now that they had both been, in some sense, resolved, I had a tremendous feeling of relief. I felt free to indulge my thoughts and my feeling for Jennifer that in a way I hadn't done since she died.

It was a bright sunny winter afternoon. The air was clear and I could see the fine detail of the landscape. I sat in the car and for the first time I felt free to go over the funeral in my mind. I thought of the large crowd of people who had come, some because it was the accepted thing to do, some to support the children and me. I have no doubt that some came because they liked Jennifer and genuinely wanted to pay their last respects to her, others out of prurience, and others to see who they'd bump into to have a chat with afterwards. People meet people at funerals that they meet nowhere else, and I have always suspected that there are some people in small communities who go to funerals to ensure there will be a reasonable crowd at their own. There were people whose attendance I particularly appreciated. Not the professionals or the prosperous traders or farmers, but the small people; a shop assistant, the County Council road worker, the man with the bald pate and the shabby overcoat, and one youngster who had been to prison more than once. Jennifer knew them all and would stop and talk to them. I had the most immense respect for the capacity she had had to see people quite naturally for who they were and not for their religion, their politics or their station in life.

I was thinking of the regard in which so many people held her, despite her well-known problem with drink. This triggered the release of emotions that I had sublimated since she died. My eyes filled and tears ran down my cheeks, so that the view disappeared. The more the tears came, the more I released my thoughts and allowed them to range freely over areas that I had been avoiding. I began to sob and soon I let go and cried uncontrollably so that my whole face was engorged. After a time I was too exhausted to cry any more and experienced a post-coital-like peace that, though it did not induce sleep, obliterated the rest of the world so that momentarily this episode of weeping had erased my grief.

The decision came easily to me and I had a wonderful feeling of freedom when I made it. I would leave the parish and the ministry. I could imagine Jennifer saying; 'At last; you should have done it years ago.' I would find some kind of work that would keep the wolf from the door and see me through to retirement. I would do anything within reason. I thought that Derek might be able to give me some kind of a job, but dismissed the idea immediately; I would sink or swim on my own. I sat and went over in my mind some of the implications of the decision; where to live, perhaps to see more of Mary and Peter, more time to read and a myriad of others. Leaving would solve all my present problems but one. I would still have to pay off the debts caused by Jennifer's drinking.

The view came into focus again through the earliest hints of dusk, so that I could see the lights of distant houses dotted around the landscape. I gave a final wipe to my eyes with my sodden handkerchief and got out of the car. It was bitterly cold. I wrapped my scarf round my neck and buttoned my coat to the top. I walked briskly along the road while a mean east wind bit into my face flushed from crying. After a few hundred yards I could bear it no longer, turned round and went back to the car. I looked in the mirror to see two bloodshot eyes and a pair of blotchy red cheeks. I started the car and drove slowly to the one person in the world to whom I could recount without awkwardness the events of the afternoon.

As I approached the lane to Kate's house I stopped the car, turned on the interior light and checked my face in the mirror. It was much the same as the last time I had looked. Kate greeted me with her usual warm smile, expecting to hear an account of my interview with the bishop. Siobhán was sleeping over with a friend. As we entered the kitchen I told Kate what had happened at the lay-by. Visibly moved, she held me. I breathed the scent of her perfume, and the warmth of her feminine form stirred something deep inside me. Kate made coffee and as we sat at the kitchen table I was totally at ease in her confidence. Reaching for a biscuit I knocked over my coffee. Kate took a dishcloth and mopped up the spill. She went to the sink, rinsed the cloth and as she wiped the table in front of me I took her hand and squeezed it. She looked straight into my eyes and smiled gently. I stood up and kissed her on the lips. She kissed me back. We looked at each other for a moment and hugged. Kate took my hand and led me to the kitchen door, across the hall and up the stairs. I stayed the night and we made love again in the morning.

About the Author

Patrick Semple is a former Church of Ireland clergyman. Patrick has had two volumes of memoirs published, and two collections of poems. He was editor of 'A Parish Adult Education Handbook,' and ghost wrote 'That Could Never Be,' a memoir by Kevin Dalton. He has had short stories published and broadcast.

Patrick currently teaches a creative writing course at National University of Ireland Maynooth, Adult Education Department and for the last three years has done public readings of his work in Kempten, Bavaria.

He has a website at *www.patricksemple.ie*

Lightning Source UK Ltd.
Milton Keynes UK
UKOW041037041012

200002UK00001B/21/P